THE LAST CANOE

JOHN CRAIG

The Last Canoe

PMA BOOKS

Canadian Cataloguing in Publication Data

Craig, John, 1921–
    The last canoe
ISBN 0-88778-196-9

1. Chippewa Indians – Fiction. I. Title.
PS8555.R23L38   C813'.5'4   C79-094759-5
PR9199.3.C73L38

Peter Martin Associates Limited
280 Bloor Street West, Suite 306, Toronto, Canada M5S 1W1

Printed in Canada by Webcom Limited

I want you to . . . open your hearts to me as children would to a father. . . . Your Great Mother, the Queen, wishes to do justice to all her children alike. . . . She wishes her red children to be happy. . . . She wishes them to live in comfort. . . .

> Lieutenant-Governor Alexander Morris, while negotiating Treaty No. 5 with the Crees and Saltaux, September 1874

The term 'person' means an individual other than an Indian.

> Indian Act of 1870

This is a novel; its characters are imaginary, its events the inventions of fiction. Yet, in a broader sense, it is all too true.

In the summer of 1933 a young Missisauga Indian did try to paddle a canoe across the Atlantic, from Peterborough, Ontario to Peterborough, England. No one ever knew why. He drowned off Anticosti Island in the Gulf of St. Lawrence.

From the beginning we have done our best to kill off the native peoples of North America by every means available to us: in the name of Christianity or progress, with imported diseases or raw whisky and cheap wine, by treaty and statute and bureaucratic memo. Often we acted with kindness.

Yet, with the exception of the Beothuks of Newfoundland, we have achieved no "final solution". Amazingly, the Indians survive; incredibly, they endure.

To avoid extinction, they have had to call upon enormous reserves of adaptability, patience, forgiveness, and lately, of guile, shrewdness and stubborn determination.

The Last Canoe is the story of how one Indian, a composite of several I have known, fought to save his people . . . and tried to show us the way.

Part One
April 1960

CHAPTER ONE

Ⅰ N a little, centuries-worn
pocket on the crest of a great block of granite protruding
from the Pre-Cambrian spine of central Ontario, Arthur
Nogawa shifted his position slightly against the raw wind
of the late April evening.

The cottagers who sometimes climbed the slopes to
pick blueberries called it the Burleigh Mountain, but,
dominating the land around though it did, the promon-
tory was no more than four hundred feet high.

The place had profound spiritual significance for the
Missisaugas. Arthur had first gone there almost fifty years
earlier to fast and to seek the personal totem that would
guide him into manhood.

This time he had climbed the craggy face as the sun
was beginning to sink on the previous day. Reaching the
peak, he had huddled there, alone, without food or water,
for a little more than twenty-four hours.

His Indian name translated roughly as Run-in-the-Rain.
A few knew him as Art. Occasionally, though never within his hearing, he was referred to as Little Arthur.

Little in stature, he was. No more than five inches over
five feet tall. Thin, almost frail looking. Bony shoulders.
Slightly sunken cheeks on either side of a somewhat
bulbous nose. Sinewy, long arms. Gnarled, worn fingers,
the top joint missing from the middle one on his left
hand.

Yet there was strength in that sparse frame, in his pierc-
ing, unblinking eyes. He had an animal-like economy of

3

movement, a seemingly boundless energy and almost appeared to blend in with, and belong to the world around him.

For thirty years or more Arthur had been acknowledged far and wide to be the best guide in all of the Kawartha Lakes. He could always find fish, even on burning hot July days when the ever-hungry gulls stayed, squawking with ill-temper, on the mirror-fringed rocks. When all else failed, Arthur would cut a sturdy sapling, tie on a short length of strong line, bait a big hook with bullfrog legs and drop it into pockets deep in the weedbeds, where the big bass and huge muskies sulked and brooded. Well-to-do American tourists booked him up a year and more in advance.

Come fall, envious hunters said that he thought like a deer, knew where they'd take cover, what they'd be feeding on, what runs they'd be using and when. If a client of his didn't get a shot at a good buck, the hunt was on Arthur, including the food.

But above all, he was renowned as a paddler. When he got into a canoe, he melded into it and became as much a part of it as the gunwales, the thwarts, the keel, the ribs, the delicate skin. Then his coiled inner strength revealed itself in perfect harmony with the frail craft he paddled. Summer after summer, he won the featured Around-Doe-Rock event at the annual McCracken's Landing regatta. Every summer some hot-shot, twenty-year-old summer resident using a wide-bladed racing paddle would be ahead at the half-way point; and every year, paddling steadily and patiently, Arthur would cut the invader down on the gruelling home-stretch. Eventually, Arthur had surrendered the title to his son, Leonard.

Now, in the spring of 1960 the chief of the Crooked Lake Missisaugas was fifty-two years old. He had been the spokesman for his people for almost two decades.

Bones wearying after his long vigil, he looked down from his perch on the lip of the Burleigh Mountain. Below him, the cabins and shacks and sheds of the village sprawled haphazardly from the base of the rock to the irregular margin of the lake, lapping and violet-blue, freed just a week before of the slate-grey ice of winter.

There, by the shore, the white clapboard house of the Indian agent, flag straight out and flapping from the peak of its pole. There, half-hidden by the still-bare sumachs, Roy Whetung's hen-house. And there, low sun glinting off the rusting soft-drink signs that formed its roof, white smoke being snatched away from the stove-pipe as Sarah made the evening meal, his own place.

In the largest, most substantial building, four men waited for Arthur to come down from the big rock. Once, not so long ago, the Crooked Lake Community Centre had been the scene of classes, meetings, square dances, birthday and anniversary parties, pot-luck suppers and bingo games. But on this April evening, the four men were almost alone. In another room Clara Whetung sat behind the desk in the library, as she did every evening, even though no one came to return or take out books anymore.

Of the four men, three formed the elected council of the Crooked Lake band, with Arthur as their chief and chairman. Ira Jacobs and Sonny Wobashung were both well over forty, like Arthur, their chief. The third, Leonard Nogawa, was Arthur's twenty-six-year-old son.

Compared to his father, Leonard was a big man—almost six feet tall, broad across the shoulders, strong looking. He had not inherited Arthur's patience; instead he was more inclined to confront issues, to take them head-on and accept the consequences.

The fourth member of the group was Jim Thorburn,

the resident agent of the Department of Indian Affairs. Thorburn, the father of four small children, was a decent enough man who cared about the Crooked Lake Indians only marginally less than he cared about keeping his job.

They were waiting there at Arthur's request. But if they did not know the specific reason for the meeting, they were all only too well aware of the problems facing the people of Crooked Lake.

Until two years before, the village had enjoyed relative prosperity. Under Arthur's guidance, the Missisaugas had made a decent living from their reservation lands, guiding for fishing in the summer, for deer in the fall and for bear in the spring. They ran trap-lines, cut pulp wood in the winter, netted bait minnows, made sweet-grass baskets for the tourists and built docks for the cottagers.

It had been a communal effort and out of it had come a communal pride. A truck bought out of band funds. A garbage dump organized. Vegetable gardens. A school house. The busy Community Centre.

It had not been easy. At first Arthur had had to fight the lethargy of his own people, and later the ponderous caution of government bureaucracy. Every expenditure of the band's own money had had to be approved by the Department, a process that could take longer than for a pike to learn to fly.

But they had done it, Arthur and the sixty families of Crooked Lake, and for some time the village had been a good place.

Then, as casually as a muskie gulps down a minnow, Ottawa had killed it. Bill Number C-137. Without warning, without having been consulted, Arthur was told that the reserve at Crooked Lake was to be incorporated into a new national park and game preserve. Two-thirds of their land would be taken away. Hunting and trapping would be prohibited.

The men in Ottawa meant well. The new park, they told each other, would provide employment for the Indians, improve their standard of living and help to bring them into the twentieth century.

But, if their intentions had been good, their ignorance was great. And what resulted was spiritual homicide—the murder of the will of the people of Crooked Lake.

The promised work in the new park had lasted for only a few months. When it dried up there was no hunting and fishing, no trap-lines, no wood-cutting to go back to. Instead, there were welfare payments. Apathy. Alcoholism. And a series of deaths along the railway tracks that fringed what was left of the reserve, and along which the Indians walked or staggered between Crooked Lake and the beer parlours and wine stores of Trentville, six miles away. The "Catawba Trail", some locals called it.

Only a handful of dull-eyed children were sent to the school house, and there was a new teacher every September. The Community Centre was an empty shell. Garbage was strewn anywhere or left to rot where it fell. Vegetable gardens were reclaimed by weeds and grasshoppers and fast-spreading sumachs. Disease and malnutrition were rampant. But worst of all was the apathy.

All of that would be on his father's mind, Leonard Nogawa knew, as it was every waking hour. Crouched up there. Cold. Hungry. Waiting for a sign. Looking for something to try, however desperate. Looking for a way out.

The Indian agent, Thorburn, pulled his package of tobacco over to him and began to roll another cigarette, turning the thin paper expertly between his stained fingers.

"How much longer do you think he'll be?" Thorburn asked the other three.

"Until he's ready," Sonny Wobashung told him.

"It's a long time to keep us waiting," Thorburn said, twisting the ends of his cigarette.

Leonard looked across at him. Much more than his father, more than the other two, he resented the presence of the agent and what he represented, even though he did not dislike the man personally. "He knows about waiting," he said.

The agent flicked a wooden match into flame with the nail of his right thumb. "I guess he does, at that," he said.

Up on the rock, the waiting was almost over for Arthur. He had watched the pale, lingering streaks of pink fade from the western sky and felt the darkness close in around and over him. Pin-points of light had come on in the Community Centre and a few of the houses. Then a half-moon had come up, dissecting the lake with a thin, coldly brilliant incision.

He knew now, certainly and with acceptance, what he must do. He had been thinking about it for months, but the long hours alone had been needed to let the idea take hold and become a reality.

Arthur stood up, stretched, the stiffness brittle and aching in the deepest sinews of his sparse frame.

"By gee," he said quietly to the adolescent moon.

Then he turned and began to work his way down the foot-scalloped, silver-shadowed path.

A few minutes later, in the Community Centre, Ira Jacobs went over to a window and looked out in the direction of the Burleigh Mountain.

"He's coming now," Jacobs said.

Leonard Nogawa and Sonny Wobashung knew it, too, although there had been no sound and nothing to be seen beyond the cramped margin of light from the window.

Jim Thorburn had been around long enough to accept such things, even though he would never understand them. The chief was coming back, all right. The question was—what word would he bring down with him?

CHAPTER TWO

WHEN he reached the Community Centre, it did not take Arthur very many words to tell them what he had in his mind. The chief's sparse shoulders were hunched slightly from exposure, and there were trickles of blood on the back of one hand where he had brushed against a last summer's raspberry cane.

The other four listened attentively as he began to speak.

He had done everything he could, he told them, to get the government in Ottawa to change its mind about the national park, to give them back their lands, to restore their former way of life. But it had been useless.

"I've been going about it the wrong way, you see," Arthur said.

"How's that?" Jim Thorburn asked, his eyes narrowed slightly with wariness.

"The treaty our ancestors signed was not with the Canadian government," Arthur explained. "It was with the British crown—with George IV, the King of England."

"Well, sure," Jim Thorburn said. "There was no Canadian government then, 'way back in 1821—not for another forty years."

Arthur nodded. "Yes," he said, "that's why I have to go to England to see the Queen."

"What?" Leonard asked incredulously.

Thorburn snorted. "Be realistic, Arthur. London's four thousand miles from here across the Atlantic Ocean."

"I know," Arthur told him. "I've looked at maps."

"Aw, that's crazy," Thorburn said.

"It's what I have to do."

"Well, I won't authorize it, not in a hundred years," the agent said. "And you can expect no help from the Department, not so much as a dime."

"I understand that," Arthur said.

"Then how in hell do you plan to get there?"

"I'll paddle," Arthur said. "In my canoe."

CHAPTER THREE

WHEN he had told them, Arthur sat watching their reactions.

Thorburn was flabbergasted, outraged. What Arthur was proposing, he said, was insane, suicidal. No canoe could survive on the North Atlantic.

Arthur knew that, knew well enough what it would be like out there. He had seen movies of the ocean. Massive, towering swells in endless procession, the troughs between them deeper than the length of a canoe, the spittle torn from the crests by demoniacal winds.

No. No man could paddle there.

Arthur's inner hope was that the authorities would not let it go that far; that his dramatic scheme would force the government into reopening the Crooked Lake question long before he was out of sight of land. Still, he was ready to try it if he had to.

He sensed, and was prepared for his son's opposition. Leonard would think that he was still playing the white man's game by the white man's rules. He would think that his father was running out, sacrificing his life for nothing. There was much bitterness and anger in Leonard. His way would be to stand and fight.

But Arthur had been around for a long time. He had spent a good part of his adult life learning to be shrewd, to compromise, to find ways around obstacles, to bend restricting regulations without breaking them, to feint in one direction and go in another.

Most of all, he knew all there was to know about survival, for himself and for his people. He had learned it the hard way, and he would play it out the hard way.

He understood very well that this was his last card—knew it as Crazy Horse, Big Bear and Geronimo had known it before him.

Arthur remembered very clearly the evening, more than ten years before, when he had first gained a working understanding of the dense tangle of treaties, royal proclamations, acts of parliament, supreme court decisions, cases, codicils, amendments and precedents governing his life and the lives of his people.

He had guided for George Sedgewick that day, as he had at least once every summer. He had first met Sedgewick years before, when neither of them had ever thought seriously about becoming middle aged or older. Sedgewick, once a struggling young lawyer, had just been appointed to the Ontario Supreme Court. His family had had a cottage on Upper Crooked Lake since early in the century, when gingerbread under the eaves had been one of the manifestations of a gracious, quieter, Victorian time.

Arthur and George were more friends than they were client and guide. They had caught many a big muskie together and shared many a shore dinner under the pines of one of the islands.

That evening, after their day of fishing, the by-then silver-haired judge had invited Arthur to stay with him for a while on the floating dock at the Sedgewick cottage. And there, over two or three beers, while the sun went down on that summer day, and the stars pierced the night sky one by one, and a whip-poor-will took up its monotonous keening, George Sedgewick had taken Arthur through the legislation which had brought the people of Crooked Lake to their present status.

He had studied the body of law because he liked Arthur and cared about his people. Most of all, he had done it because he was a man who was genuinely concerned with justice, as frequently distinct from jurisprudence.

Although personally appalled and professionally embarrassed by what he had discovered, the judge had laid it on the line for Arthur, simply and honestly, quoting sources when called for and reciting the whole history in clear, organized, chronological fashion. By the time he had finished, most of the lights had winked out in the island cottages and the dawn was closer than the dusk.

"By gee," Arthur had said then, "you must be a pretty good lawyer to make me understand all that stuff."

"It's terrible, Arthur," Sedgewick had said. "It's immoral and it's inhuman and it's a mockery—but it's also the law. I thought it might help you some to know."

A couple of weeks later the judge had sent him a thin sheaf of photocopied pages summarizing the gist of the documents he had talked about that evening and night. Arthur had read them again and again, the sheets of paper becoming ever more thumb-marked, until he had assimilated every sentence, every clause, every word.

The legal extinction of the Missisaugas of Crooked Lake began with the signing of a treaty in October 1821, on the site of what later became the small city of Trentville, Ontario:

> We, the Principal Chiefs of the Missisauga Nation, for Ourselves and on behalf of our Nation, do hereby consent and agree with Richard Howson, Esquire, Deputy Superintendant-General of Indian Affairs, on behalf of His Majesty, George IV, that for the consideration of one thousand pounds, in goods at the Montreal price . . . we do hereby cede, release, and yield up all the lands bordering the body of water generally known as Crooked Lake.

14

A later paragraph began promisingly:

> His Majesty further agrees that the said Indians shall have the right to pursue their avocations of hunting and fishing throughout the tract surrendered. . . .

But it ended by denying any such guarantee:

> . . . subject to such regulations as may from time to time be enacted by His Government, and saving and excepting such tracts as may from time to time be required for settlement, mining, lumbering or other purpose.

The 1821 Treaty concluded with a number of ornate English army signatures set against the crudely drawn totems of Missisauga Chiefs—Sagasway, Paymekawnawassegay, Nawbowe, Tommago.

A century later the notion that Treaty Indians enjoyed special rights to hunt and fish on their reservation lands was laid to rest by Mr. Justice Riddell in the case of *Sero vs. Gault* (50, OLR 27, 1921):

> The law since 1826 has never been in doubt. . . . I can find no justification for the supposition that any Indians are exempt from the general law . . . or ever were.

The legal precedent for this ruling had been established long ago, before in fact the treaty with the Missisaugas had ever been signed, by Chief Justice Marshall of the U.S. Supreme Court (*Worcester vs. Georgia*, 1821):

> Power, war, conquest give rights which, after possession, are conceded by the world . . . and can never be controverted by those on whom they descend.

That Indian lands could be reclaimed by the Crown was made clear in a decision taken by the Privy Council in *St. Catharines Milling vs. the Queen* in 1889:

The lands reserved are expressly stated to be parts of Our dominions and territories; and it is declared to be the will and pleasure of the Sovereign that *"for the present"* they shall be reserved for the use of the Indians. . . .

Arthur knew that it was the phrase "for the present" that really counted. What it added up to was the harsh fact that the Indians really had no rights at all. Even the famous phrase "as long as the sun shines and the rivers run", although spoken often by the treaty-makers, had never been written down, and was thus, as Sedgewick had told him, of no significance.

But, thanks to the lawyer, Arthur had at least understood what he was up against. Now, ten years later, he had taken out the old documents again, pouring over them night after night by the yellow light from a coal oil lamp. They—and the time he had spent on the Burleigh Mountain—had led him to his decision to go to London to see the Queen. Or to start out, at least, with the expectation that public indignation might embarrass the authorities into stopping him.

Now he waited, answering as best he could, while the opposition of Leonard and Thorburn ran its course.

"So, you're determined to go ahead with this foolishness?" Thorburn asked.

"Oh, yes," Arthur said.

He had no wish to die, and he did not want to leave his wife Sarah, or Leonard, or his daughter-in-law Nona, or his new grandson John. But it was what had to be done.

The meeting ended soon after that. But Arthur knew the resistance was still there. Leonard would argue with him through long hours yet to come. And the agent would be on the phone to Ottawa first thing the next morning to ask for further instructions.

But it was over for now.

"When will you want to leave?" Dan Jacobs asked as the five of them got up to leave. Neither he nor Sonny Wobashung had raised any objection.

"As soon as we can get the canoe ready," Arthur told him.

"Yes," Sonny said, "we will need to make it stronger."

At the door Arthur waited for the others to step outside, then switched off the lights and closed the door behind him.

CHAPTER FOUR

WHEN it broke, the news of Arthur's plan stirred up considerable excitement in the district around Crooked Lake and gained some attention from farther afield. It was mentioned briefly in newspapers as distant as New York and San Francisco and even earned two paragraphs in Moscow's *Pravda*. The *Toronto Telegram* ran a feature article under the banner, "INDIAN PADDLER TO CHALLENGE ATLANTIC", which omitted any reference to the political background and left the impression that the voyage was being undertaken as a personal feat of derring-do. The Canadian Broadcasting Corporation sent a crew to Crooked Lake to film a segment for its Sunday night public affairs television program.

Locally, reactions fell into three main categories. One group, probably the largest, was inclined to shrug it off as the kind of childish, irresponsible act to be expected of Indians; when it came time, he wouldn't go, they said.

There were others, though, who were genuinely concerned that a man, any man, should be forced to such a desperate measure to gain justice for his people. They included the members of a Unitarian congregation, the local of a national trade union, a young lawyer, a music teacher *cum* amateur archaelogist and Baz Dinneen, the editor of the *Trentville Daily Examiner*.

Throughout the late spring and early summer Dinneen, a flabby, sloppily dressed, sixty-year-old hulk of a man, used his editorial columns to flay the provincial and federal governments for their sell-out of the Crooked Lake people.

The Dinneen-led liberals held meetings, organized a public rally and generally stirred up enough controversy to coerce nervous officials in both Toronto and Ottawa into making statements that the Crooked Lake situation was "under investigation".

The third group, spear-headed by Trentville mayor Orville Dennison, saw in Arthur's proposed voyage the perfect occasion for a civic celebration and tourist attraction. The local Chamber of Commerce and the Motel and Hotel Operators' Association quickly jumped on the bandwagon. The first of several press releases from this faction was made available towards the end of May.

Under the heading "EPIC VOYAGE TO START JULY 1ST", the copy urged everyone to "be on hand to give the Chief a great send-off!". Plans were well under way to make the day "a great one in the history of Trentville". There would be floats and marching bands, and many dignitaries, elected officials and "personalities from TV, stage, screen and the world of sports" had already indicated that they would be on hand. A huge crowd was expected, with "many visitors from far and near".

Arthur took it all in his stride. The tawdry exploitation might be hard to swallow, but he would tolerate almost anything that might draw attention to the plight of his people.

Meanwhile, there was the canoe to get ready. Sonny Wobashung and Dan Jacobs, and sometimes one or two others, worked on it with him. Once a photographer from the *Trentville Examiner* came out to take pictures. On weekends, an occasional early cottager boated down to see what was going on. But usually they worked without distractions.

They had set the canoe up across a couple of saw-horses behind the Community Centre, not far from the shore of the lake. It was a standard model, built in the classic fashion of the early twentieth century. Sixteen feet long,

19

it had short decks at the bow and stern. The flat ribs, an inch and a half wide and set the same distance apart, went out horizontally from the keel, then curved upwards to meet the ash gunwales. There were three thwarts, one more or less in the middle, the other two each about a quarter of the way from either end.

It was a fragile craft, yet in proper hands it could survive an incredible battering from wind and waves. But to do so, man and boat had to become one in the struggle against the elements, their combined balance always in harmony, their reactions instinctive and complementary. Arthur knew the centre of gravity had to be kept low; in big storms that would swamp power yachts and merchant vessels an Indian paddler might survive by lying flat along the keel and waiting for the wind to blow itself out. Though not, of course, on the North Atlantic.

Arthur and the others sanded every square inch of the canoe by hand, then gave it several coats of varnish inside and a new external skin of red paint. To give the vessel greater lateral strength, they fashioned lengths of seasoned white oak and lashed them between the gunwales with lengths of sinew. Old Clarence Smoke and his wife Lenora made a tarpaulin from a piece of tent canvas and stretched it between the bow deck and the front thwart to shelter Arthur's food and other supplies.

And under the deck at the stern Dan Jacobs fitted a small, well-protected shelf where Arthur would keep his carefully wrapped diary. Long experience in dealing with government departments had taught Arthur the importance of keeping records, and he hoped that a daily chronicle of his voyage might prove useful—should he survive.

"Anyway, it will give me something to do," he said.

"You'll have plenty to do," his wife Sarah told him. Her heart grew heavier as the days passed, but she, too, knew that it was what Arthur had to do. She could only make it as good for him as possible and be strong in dignity when the time for parting came.

Leonard was unable to accept his father's decision as gracefully. To him the plan was an exercise in futility and humiliation, and there could be no dignity in it. He thought of organizing a protest march to Ottawa, but realized bitterly that the people of the reserve were too apathetic to carry out such a community effort. He argued with Arthur, tried to reason with him, even pleaded with him. All to no avail. Finally, he retreated into silence; he would no longer oppose the undertaking, but neither would he participate in it. He did not come by to see how the preparation of the canoe was progressing, and he stayed away each time Nona asked Arthur and Sarah over for supper. On those occasions, watching his infant grandson John playing in his crib in Nona and Leonard's house, Arthur understood, though he was saddened by Leonard's absence.

Sarah was the one who thought of making pemmican as emergency food for the voyage. Compact and rich in food energy, it would keep well and take up relatively little space in the canoe. She remembered the recipe as told to her by her grandmother—venison, suet, maple syrup and berries pressed into cakes and dried. It was the first time pemmican had been prepared at Crooked Lake in almost a century.

From its tentative beginnings, the spring of that year swelled into summer. The earth, released finally and impatient, smelled of old death and new life. Pickerel swarmed in the thousands at the mouth of Eel's Creek and below the Burleigh rapids. Partridge drummed and strutted along fallen trees. Fiddlehead ferns unfurled delicately in shadowed glens. Migrating geese filled the sky with their cacaphony. Frogs chorused in the swamps.

21

May came. More and more cottagers returned each weekend. Shutters were taken down. Leaves were raked and burned. Docks, damaged by the spring break-up, were contemplated ruefully. Flower and vegetable gardens were dug and planted. Boats were slipped into water that still remembered the icy grip of winter.

Trilliams and dog-tooth violets blossomed. Clouds of insidious black flies temporarily halted work on the canoe. Spawning muskies moved into shallow, stump-margined bays, where they lay side by side, their great backs warmed by the late spring sun. The poplar leaves rippled like gossamer silver coins in the breeze.

Then June. A few minutes before midnight on the second day of the new month, a forty-three-year old Crooked Lake Indian named Henry Penabuishene was cut in two by the wheels of a freight engine about a mile east of the reserve. His was the third such death along the Catawba Trail since the beginning of the year. As was usual in such cases, no inquest was ordered by the county coroner.

By the time Henry died, the canoe was as ready as Arthur and the others could make it. As ready as a canoe could be for the North Atlantic.

By then, too, Mayor Orville Dennison's promotional campaign was in full swing. July 1 was going to be a big day in the history of Trentville. The parade, His Honour enthused, would be "a mile long, anyway—maybe closer to two miles!". A number of local merchants and businessmen had come forward to donate equipment and supplies for Arthur's voyage, and their gifts were on display in the lobby of the new city hall:

* SAIL DONATED BY TRENTVILLE MARINA *
PORTABLE REFRIGERATOR COURTESY OF
GRAFTON APPLIANCES * THE CHIEF WILL

22

SLEEP ON AN INFLATABLE MATTRESS FROM
LEACHMAN'S SURPLUS STORE * CASE OF
COKES, HAP'S VARIETY *

And in the park which housed the war memorial and
backed onto the football field of the Trentville high
school, the Junior Chamber of Commerce erected a billboard. On it, in vivid colours, was a schematic map of
the route Arthur would follow: the necklace of lakes and
rivers down to Lake Ontario, then on to Kingston and
the beginning of the St. Lawrence, Montreal, Quebec
City, the great river broadening into the Gulf, Anticosti
Island, Newfoundland and finally the Atlantic. There
was a blue star for Trentville and a red one, slightly larger,
for London, England. At the lower right-hand corner,
there was a poorly drawn caricature of an Indian, complete with beads and feathers, paddling a birch bark canoe. At the top, in block letters, ran the caption: "Follow the Chief's Progress—His Position Plotted Daily!"

It was all completely abhorrent to those who looked
upon the voyage as a tragedy and the need for it as an
indictment of a cruel injustice. And there was reason to
feel encouragement in their efforts. Some of Baz Dinneen's
editorials were picked up and reprinted in other newspapers. Prayers were offered in several local churches. A
rally in the Trentville Civic Centre was attended by over
four hundred citizens, some merely curious, but most
committed to the Crooked Lake cause. And donations
poured in to help finance the campaign.

Best of all, the federal and provincial representatives
of the Trentville-Crooked Lake electoral districts both
went on record as supporting a reopening of the case.

On Parliament Hill, young MP Frank O'Leary issued a
statement that he had "the assurance of the Minister responsible as to his personal determination to find a just
solution to the Crooked Lake question".

23

And at Toronto's Queen's Park, veteran MPP Gordon Hastings told a reporter from the *Globe and Mail* that he would "leave no stone unturned" in his efforts to "see that Chief Nogawa and his people are treated fairly".

Both were honourable men; at the time both believed in what they said.

In Trentville Baz Dinneen believed that they were beginning to win the battle. "Even if they let him go," he told a newspaper colleague over coffee at the DeLuxe Café, "they'll have to haul him back long before he ever sees the Atlantic. There's too much public pressure to let him die."

June blossomed, and wilted.

On the eve of his departure, Arthur and Sarah had supper at their daughter-in-law's. The red canoe had been trucked to Trentville by then and was floating, snubbed at bow and stern, alongside the government wharf in Little Lake Park, near the centre of town. A patrolman was assigned by Police Chief Ira Lennox to keep the curious from getting too close to it.

For their final meal together, Nona had prepared Arthur's favourite, slapjacks, a kind of dumplings made from wild rice flour, floated on a rabbit stew.

As usual the little grandson, John, played in his crib. But unlike the other times, Leonard was there. They ate the food, finishing off with stewed rhubarb, cake and tea.

It was strange because the finality of it, though imminent, was not yet real, not yet there. It was all still familiar, as it had always been. Nona found herself thinking of chores awaiting her, little things like putting a patch on the elbow of Leonard's brown windbreaker, and had to remind herself that Arthur would no longer be there when the time came to perform them; that he would, in all likelihood, never share a meal with them again.

Afterwards, Arthur and Leonard took their tea out onto the screened-in porch, while Sarah and Nona did the dishes. The two men sat across from each other at an old, splay-legged card table. June bugs beat their wings and died against the wire mesh enclosing the porch.

"Are you afraid?" Leonard asked his father.

Arthur looked taken aback by the question.

"Don't you know?" he asked. "Indians aren't supposed to ever get scared."

Leonard laughed. "No—or feel pain."

"That's right," Arthur said. "I haven't thought about it much yet. I will be, though. I know that."

Leonard went into the next room and returned with little John. Arthur's grandson lay across his father's lap, cradled by one arm, playing with a plastic rattle.

"I wonder what kind of a world he'll grow up in," Leonard said.

"Oh, he'll be all right," Arthur said. "I used to think about that when you were his age."

The baby's little face broke into a smile as Leonard tickled him lightly under one tiny arm.

"It's not getting any better, though," Leonard said. "I had it pretty good when I was a kid."

"Teach him about the things you know," Arthur said. "The animals, the fish, the seasons, the old ways."

"There isn't much room left for those things anymore," Leonard said. "Maybe I should teach him how to fight instead."

"He'll learn how to fight, if he has to," Arthur said quietly.

Leonard nodded, not really convinced. "I suppose so," he said. "We used to know, our people."

25

"We still know, most of us," Arthur said. "Only now it's a different kind of fighting . . . a squirrel against a bear."

"Do you think they'll stop you?" Leonard asked.

Arthur considered the question carefully before answering. "They will see that that is the right thing to do," he said then.

"But will they do it?"

"I don't know," Arthur said.

"In time?"

"I don't know."

They fell silent then for some seconds. The baby had fallen asleep in Leonard's lap.

"If they don't," Arthur said, "do the best you can for him and your mother and Nona—for the others, too."

"I will," Leonard told him.

"It'll be harder on them than on me," Arthur said. "At least I'll know what's happening."

"It will be hard on everybody," Leonard said.

Sarah and Nona came to the door.

"It's time we were going," Sarah said. "Tomorrow will be a long day."

Arthur got up. "It will," he said.

They said their good-nights at the kitchen door, a ritual carried over from other, ordinary times.

"Thank you for a nice supper."

"Glad you could come."

Arthur and Sarah left.

Leonard put the baby, still sleeping, into his crib, then joined Nona at the window of their house. They stood close together, his arm around her waist, looking out into the patient summer twilight, watching as the two shadowed figures walked along the path.

CHAPTER FIVE

AS the mayor had promised, the Dominion Day parade was a mile long, more or less. Held every July 1, as Trentville's way of marking the nation's birthday, the 1960 edition was designed to centre around Arthur's departure.

The parade consisted of a couple of dozen floats fashioned mainly from crèpe paper, some featuring maple leaves, several with Indian themes, none notably inspired. The local militia turned out in a long column of battledress khaki, swinging along behind the 57th Regimental Band. The fire department was represented by the town's new hook-and-ladder rig, its siren wailing intermittently. A Dixieland band played from the bed of a stake truck. A car with loudspeakers on its roof urged one and all to attend the "gala Kiwanis Club carnival" in the fair grounds that night.

It was the usual small-town parade. Baton-twirling majorettes. Kilted, red-faced bagpipers. A festooned city bus. Gaps. Delays. A fife-and-drum band. Miss Central Ontario of 1960.

The mayor and the other dignitaries brought up the rear, waving to the spectators from open convertibles. Frank O'Leary was on hand, and Gordon Hastings. Arthur was supposed to arrive in a fifth car, but he failed to show up at the marshalling area.

Some watched the parade from the sidewalk as it came down the main street, but most congregated in the vicinity of the wharf, where it ended. By eleven o'clock, an hour before Arthur was scheduled to leave, the waterfront area was jammed, and the overflow spilled out towards Cemetery Point.

Whole families. Old men alone. Old women in pairs. Teenagers with portable radios. Parents with infant children. Some carrying lawn chairs. Some with blankets. Many with picnic hampers. Most with cameras.

Off shore, all manner of boats drifted or bobbed at anchor: sleek cabin cruisers, houseboats, homemade punts, canoes, runabouts, dinghies and even a catamaran.

The immediate wharf area was like a miniature midway. A couple of souvenir stands were doing a steady business. Kids were lined up at both the small merry-go-round and the pony ride. Customers were four and five deep around the refreshment booths. Hot dogs and hamburgers frying. Mustard. Onions. Candy floss. Litter barrels spilled over. There was an acute shortage of toilets.

At one side of the wharf a section had been roped off around a hastily constructed platform, gaudy with red, white and blue bunting, its back edge rimmed with folding chairs. Near the front stood a microphone stand, and cables snaked across the weeds and grasshoppers to a sound truck.

Fifty feet away Arthur's canoe waited, its ropes looped around big iron bollards that originally had been meant for steamboats. It looked almost ridiculously frail there, riding on the dead calm water, the hot sun glinting off its fresh red paint and varnish. The canvas tarpaulin was rigged in place over the forward third of the open hull. A paddle was leaning against the middle thwart, and a second was lashed below the opposite gunwale. There was a napsack and some odds and ends of gear on the floorboards in the stern section—a bailing tin, an iron frying pan, a hand line for trolling, wrapped around a piece of board that had been notched at both ends, and

28

Arthur's maps—oil company road maps of Ontario and Quebec.

At the opposite end of the wharf, Arthur crouched down in the shade of an old, sagging boathouse, from where he could keep an eye on the canoe. With him were Sarah, Leonard, Nona, Sonny Wobashung and old Clarence Smoke.

"They givin' you a pretty good send-off, anyways," Sonny said.

Arthur smiled. "Oh, my, yes," he said.

They didn't talk much. There was nothing much left to say except good-bye.

The final car in the parade inched its way through the crowd and drew up beside the others at the back of the wharf. The politicians got out and stood in a little group, looking uncertain and somewhat self-conscious until the mayor led the way to the steps up to the platform. A police constable untied the rope to let them through, then retied it behind them. The official party milled around for a moment before sorting itself out and finding seats on the folding chairs.

A young man from the mayor's office went over to the boathouse and asked Arthur to join the group on the platform.

"No," Arthur told him. "You fellas go ahead. Say thanks for me, though."

When the man had gone, Arthur spoke a few words to each of the others, Sarah being the last. There were no handshakes, no kisses, no signs of emotion. Then he walked over and sat on the edge of the wharf near the canoe. He was dressed in a grey flannel shirt, buttoned at the wrists in the Indian fashion in spite of the July heat. His green work pants were held up by faded suspenders, and he wore the old straw fedora he never seemed to be without in the summer months.

29

Mayor Dennison, slightly annoyed that Arthur had declined his invitation, went over to the microphone. It squealed as he adjusted it to his height, then emitted a loud and steady hum. Some in the crowd hooted and whistled while a workman located the source of the trouble.

"Distinguished guests, friends, welcome visitors. . ." His Honour began after the delay. He talked for five minutes about the reason for the celebration, the sense of civic pride Arthur's decision inspired and how the voyage would "put Trentville on the map". A number of other speakers followed: Gordon Hastings, Frank O'Leary, the president of the Chamber of Commerce, two local aldermen. The speeches were well laced with phrases like "historic occasion", "epic voyage" and "saga of the sea". None of the speakers mentioned the possibility—the hope—that Arthur's trip might be cancelled. None suggested that the authorities responsible were mad to let Arthur go.

Observing the scene from the shade of a nearby oak tree, Baz Dinneen shook his massive head in disbelief and indignation. "My God," he said to no one in particular, "they're all talking as if he might actually make it— cheering him on, instead of trying to stop him!"

As the ceremonies drew to a close a frail, elderly clergyman moved to the microphone and pronounced a benediction, asking that Arthur be protected "from the perils of the sea".

In the hush that followed, part of the crowd became aware of a sound so totally alien to their time and place that it sent a chill along the spines of those who heard it. A low, nasal, throbbingly repetitive chanting: *"Hunna-hun-hey . . . hunna-hun-hey . . . hunna-hun-hey. . . ."*

Puzzled eyes peered in the direction of the sound. What they saw was a very old Indian, an ancient man of wrinkled, leathery face and twisted, wasted body crouched down in the dirt behind one of the temporarily abandoned hot-dog stands. Emaciated. Ugly. Matted, dead hair. Filthy. Shaking a turtle-shell rattle with scrawny hands in a beat out of the mists of time.

His presence had a strange effect upon the people. Some shuffled back a step or two. Some sought a hand to hold. Some reached out protectively towards their children. A few giggled nervously.

None could recall ever having seen the old man before, and none of them knew that he was a *shaman,* a practicing member of the ancient medicine society of the Mississaugas, a man who lived with the spirit world and had the power to call down the dreaded curse of the Bear Walk. No one on that hot July day ever dreamed that such things were still part of the reality of life at Crooked Lake, just a few miles from their town.

Recovering quickly, though still flustered, Mayor Dennison motioned indignantly for someone to remove the unsightly and unwelcome interloper. He would say later that he thought it was "just another drunken Indian". A uniformed police constable started in that direction but stopped after a few seconds, not knowing what to do next. Then Arthur cut across in front of him.

The chief walked slowly, seemingly oblivious to his surroundings, towards the hunched figure of the old man. When he got there, he stood for a moment, then crouched down on one knee in front of the *shaman.*

The crowd, watching with a strange fascination, became almost completely hushed. No one coughed. No children shouted. No babies cried. The small merry-go-round, with its horses bobbing up and down, coasted to a stop. The music of the calliope petered out.

Arthur's obvious obeisance in the presence of the

ancient *shaman* lent a powerful, if little understood reality and a strange dignity to what had been just a bizarre and vaguely disturbing incident. Where once the old Indian had seemed ridiculous and somewhat frightening, he now seemed to be part of something that was timeless and profound—and totally alien to their experience.

In the sustained silence the *shaman*'s guttural chant, dominant now, echoed out across the little lake. "*Hunna-hun-hey . . . hunna-hun-hey . . . hunna-hun-hey. . . .*"

Arthur knelt there for perhaps a minute and a half, but the passing seconds seemed much longer to those looking on. For Arthur, it was an interlude without temporal limits, a time out of time. No words were exchanged, no rituals carried out. The *shaman*, he knew, was not there to bestow a blessing on the voyage that was about to begin, nor to cast down omens and portents as to its outcome. No, the *shaman* was there to represent and verify the oneness of his people, the Missisaugas, their past, present and future. And that was very important to Arthur in the task he had undertaken, more important even than the fact that those dearest to him were there in the shade of the boathouse.

"*Hunna-hun-hey . . . hunna-hun-hey. . . .*"

When he had absorbed all that was to be taken from the spirit world of the *shaman*, he stood up, gracefully and with pride.

At that moment the spell was broken. Scattered coughing broke out. A little boy yelled as he threw a ball in the general direction of his friend. Babies began to cry once more.

Arthur turned away and went straight back across the wharf. He bent down to untie the bow rope of the canoe.

"He's going!" the mayor said, suddenly realizing that the big moment was at hand.

32

"Get the band! Get the band!" an aide on the platform shouted.

Arthur freed the stern rope, then stepped down into the canoe, settling himself comfortably on the middle thwart, one leg tucked back under it, the other, bent easily at the knee, out in front of him. He picked up the paddle, used the blade to push the canoe away from the wharf, then took a couple of quick, choppy strokes to bring the bow around to face across the small lake. Then the paddle seemed to become an extension of his own body, the blade slicing into the water like a knife on each entry, almost skimming the surface on each return.

The people in the crowd began to clap and cheer, the applause spreading as the canoe pulled away. Many of the anchored boats blew their whistles, tooted their horns, sounded their sirens.

Standing in a row, Sarah, Leonard, Nona, Sonny Wobashung and Clarence Smoke watched silently as the distance between the wharf and the canoe steadily increased. So did Baz Dinneen. And Jim Thorburn.

The members of the band of the 57th Regiment scurried to form up, frantically leafing through their books of orchestrations and swinging into "All the Nice Girls Love a Sailor", followed by "A Life on the Ocean Wave".

The clarinets and trumpets, the tubas and trombones and triangles drowned out the turtle-shell rattle of the ancient Mississaga *shaman*.

The pile of donated goods—the sail, the inflatable mattress, the portable refrigerator, the case of Cokes—had been left behind, neatly stacked on the cement wall of the wharf.

The canoe continued on its course, growing ever smaller. Occasionally the brilliant noon-day sun glinted off the blade of Arthur's paddle.

Twenty minutes later the man and the canoe were

33

gone around Cemetery Point, where the small lake became a river again.

CHAPTER SIX

AFTER Dominion Day, Trentville settled down to enjoy the fruits of another ripening summer. On the American Fourth of July holiday, campers and cottagers poured into the district from south of the border until it seemed that half the cars parked on the main street bore licence plates from New York, New Jersey, West Virginia, Pennsylvania, Ohio, Illinois and Michigan.

Merchants pushed up their prices, as they did at the beginning of every July, and were glad to be serving the well-heeled summer visitors again. The liquor store broadened its variety of imported wines. Pavilions, their shutters propped open to admit the cool, evening breezes, once more throbbed to the music of Saturday night dances. After dark, men and boys prowled lawns and golf courses with lanterns, plucking dew worms to sell to bait dealers.

On island-dotted Upper Crooked Lake, the summer season moved into high gear. Barbecues sizzled and smoked. Successful executives and their well-tanned wives stirred very dry martinis, took moisture-beaded cans of beer from refrigerators, swirled the ice cubes in gin and tonics. The regatta committee of the cottagers' association held its first meeting. Bare skin burned, baked, peeled and browned under the hot sun. Horseshoes clanged off iron pegs. Hot-dogging water-skiers crisscrossed the sparkling waters from dawn to dusk. Kids shouted "Watch me!" as they belly-flopped from docks and diving boards.

35

Through the weed-rimmed narrows that led to the lower lake, life went on more or less as usual on the Crooked Lake reserve. Jim Thorburn struggled to keep up with his paper work. Nona swept, washed, cooked and looked after her baby. Wilbur Pemedash slashed his wife's face with a broken beer bottle. Leonard worked long hours, leaving in the early morning and returning in the late evening, to finish Dr. Clarkson's new boathouse. He worked harder, Nona knew, than was required of him.

Sarah Nogawa found it hard to take much interest in cooking just for herself. A pie would last her a week. She boiled wild strawberries down into jam on her wood stove, forcing from her mind the dreadful likelihood that Arthur would not be there to share it with her come winter.

In Trentville Baz Dinneen and the others who shared his views went on with their campaign to bring Arthur back. Things continued to look promising: over a thousand people signed a petition they circulated; there was still money in the campaign kitty; Frank O'Leary and Gordon Hastings reaffirmed their determination to see justice done at Crooked Lake.

"Jesus, they're slow," Baz said to a fellow supporter. "But there's got to be some word soon—they can't let him go much farther."

At that time the billboard in the park showed the position of the canoe as only a foot or so, perhaps thirty miles, south and east of the blue Trentville star.

CHAPTER SEVEN

FOR the first few days, it didn't seem like anything special or very different to Arthur. He knew that each paddle-stroke was taking him farther away from Sarah and the rest of what had been his life, but in the beginning the country looked familiar, much like his own.

A lot of it was still forest, with, here and there, patchwork farms, seldom prosperous looking, for the soil was thin and grudging, little more than a dusting of sand between the quartz and granite outcroppings of the Great Shield. Piles of stones in the fields. Split-cedar rail fences. A few black-and-white pasturing cows.

The canoe did not lack company as it followed the bends of the meandering Otonabee. Traffic was heavy on that stretch of the waterway: sauntering houseboats, with swim suits and laundry hung out to dry; big, hard-driving cabin cruisers that left the red and black buoys bobbing in their wakes and forced Arthur to bring the bow around so as to meet the swells head-on; speeding outboards, slapping into the waves; a chugging government tug, towing a scow—all competed for space in the narrow channel of water.

Now and then someone waved to him—a young woman poised on a diving board, a man still fishing from an old, white skiff or a party of tourists looking down from a steel bridge. But although there were plenty of people around, Arthur felt no desire for company or talk, not when he would, so soon, be truly alone.

The numerous locks slowed him down, as he had

known they would. He portaged around some, waited at others to lock through with other, larger craft. But in spite of the obstacles, he was putting ten or twelve miles a day behind his paddle. When night fell, he made camp wherever he could find an unoccupied point or small island, sleeping under the tarpaulin or under the overturned canoe when it rained.

At the end of the third day he reached the weedy bay from which the Trent River begins its journey south to Lake Ontario. That evening, in the lingering July twilight, he made the first entry in his diary.

July 3:
Well, pretty good so far. Had a few aches, but mostly better now. Caught a 'lunge this afternoon (pretty little!) and had it for supper. This is the easy part, I guess, along here. Wonder how things are back home? Don't suppose I'll get much news.

After another three days, he had finished with the Trent and made a good beginning on his long journey to the east.

July 6:
Started out into the big lake this afternoon. Not as bad as I expected. They call this the Bay of Quinte. The shore comes pretty close on both sides, and there isn't much wind. A man on a big boat told me that it will be like this most of the way to Kingston. Only a couple of open stretches to worry about. That's good!

But Lake Ontario was not prepared to let him slip by so unmarked.

July 8:
Luck bad. Real strong east wind yesterday and today. Hard paddling in big swells. Just about swamp-

ed four or five times. Had to get down on bottom and let her drift. Got washed up on shore just before dark. Canoe and me all right but plenty wet. Think I'm on Amherst Island.

July 9:
Been here all day. Have never seen waves like it—some a lot taller than me. Not the ocean yet, though. There's a glow over east that must be Kingston. Don't know when I'll be able to get over there. Had some pemmican tonight. Just have to wait—that's all I can do.

It was the better part of still another day before the storm finally began to blow itself out, and he could get started again. The wind, having shifted half-way around the compass, was driving in hard from the west under clearing skies, and the canoe raced down the big combers like a playful otter on a mud bank.

But Arthur knew that he could handle anything that might come up from astern. What concerned him was the two days he had lost. In the weeks and months ahead, there would come a time, he knew, when he would give a lot to have them back.

CHAPTER EIGHT

AT the beginning, while
Arthur was still in the district where the story of his voyage was generally well known, it was easy enough for those who were interested to keep track of his progress. Part-time newspaper correspondents, called "stringers", along his route kept their eyes open for the red canoe and phoned in reports when they spotted it passing by. Ordinary citizens down-river told relatives in Trentville that they had seen him, and a local television station sent a cameraman out to shoot some footage. Using reports from various sources, the custodian of the map in the park was able to move his miniature red canoe a couple of inches each day.

But it only took about two weeks for Arthur Nogawa to be all but forgotten, even in Trentville. Once he moved out into Lake Ontario, there could be no more regular media coverage: much of the time he was too far from shore to be noticed, and the farther away he got, the less likely people were to know about, or look for him.

Arthur made contact only when he needed a few supplies, and then he felt no reason to identify himself. There was no phone at Crooked Lake, apart from the one in the agent's residence. He wrote to Sarah every week or ten days, but it was not in her nature to share the contents of his letters with anyone outside of the family.

Thus, by the time July reached its zenith, Arthur had pretty well slipped from mind, as well as from sight. The *Trentville Examiner* ran a wire service photo of the red canoe sharing a lock with an enormous grain carrier, over the caption "The ant and the elephant". On July 16, and again a few days later, there was a brief report that he had been spotted near Morrisburg on the St. Lawrence. But so little news filtered back that the billboard map showed his position as unchanged for days at a time, and soon passersby stopped bothering to glance at it.

Even at Crooked Lake most people quickly got used to Arthur's absence and lost any interest in his progress that they originally might have had. Under the hot sun, the reserve dozed on in its physical and spiritual hangover. Sonny Wobashung and Dan Jacobs got a few days work guiding for fishing parties out of Sunset Lodge on the upper lake, but none of the other men even bothered to take out licences. Leonard continued with his building, working alone because he could not find a reliable helper. The humid weather produced one of the best crops of blueberries in recent memory, but only a few had the initiative to go up on the ridges to pick them. Clara Whetung finally accepted the fact that there was no point in going to the library anymore, now that no one came. Flies swarmed around the piles of randomly strewn garbage.

More than anyone else, Baz Dinneen saw what was happening, saw with increasing frustration, then anger and finally panic that time was dwindling away. He realized for the first time that Arthur might actually be permitted to die . . . to just slip away into oblivion.

The big editor worked still harder in his efforts to get something done about it, cornering anyone who would listen to him, corresponding with everyone who could possibly help in the fight, flogging and challenging the bureaucrats and politicians in his editorial columns. A few others, too, remained committed to the campaign, but several of the original supporters fell by the wayside, some from boredom, some with new enthusiasm for other causes, some resigned to the conviction that nothing more could be done. The trickle of financial contributions dried up, and at a meeting during the third week of July, fewer than thirty people attended.

A couple of days later, Baz Dinneen boarded the morning train to Ottawa, determined not to leave the capital without getting a firm commitment that Arthur would be stopped. He was there for a little more than forty-eight hours, by the end of which he was on the brink of complete exhaustion. During that time he talked to more people than he could remember, requested appointments, demanded interviews, dragged his huge and protesting body from one government office to another. He became steadily more dishevelled, pleading, arguing, protesting, questioning, flattering and occasionally shouting.

By and large, he was treated well enough. Almost all of the politicians and civil servants he met were courteous, at least at first; the majority were co-operative; many were sympathetic. He was invited to lunch in the parliamentary dining room by Frank O'Leary, the member from Trentville-Crooked Lake. The Minister of Indian Affairs was in Calgary, but Dinneen spent three-quarters of an hour with one of his executive assistants. He had drinks with a senior administrator at the Chateau Laurier and managed to see another half-dozen high-ranking officials.

They all were interested in what he had to say. They all agreed that important principles were at stake. They all expressed admiration for Arthur Nogawa and what he was doing. They all appeared to be on top of the situation. They all, in almost identical words, insisted that "the Crooked Lake question" was "a long way from being closed". To a man, they confirmed their confidence in the system and their belief that justice would be done "through the proper channels".

When it was over, the Trentville editor was impressed by the number of intelligent, hard-working men he had met. Decent men. Concerned men.

Thus, as he boarded the train to go back home, he should have felt considerably reassured.

And yet, for all the talk, no one had given him a firm promise or even a hint of a deadline.

He realized then that those intelligent, hard-working, decent and concerned men had a lot more on their minds than the fate of one short, stubborn Indian.

"Can't rush it, old boy," one of them had told him, not at all unkindly. "These things take time—always have, always will."

But with August only a handful of days away, time was Arthur's enemy, not his friend.

CHAPTER NINE

BY the time Baz Dinneen returned home from Ottawa, Arthur had already come to the beginning of the white water. There was to be an awful lot of it, more than he had ever dreamed existed in the world. In time he would come to think that the St. Lawrence was just one long rapids—dangerous in its quieter stretches, demoniacal where the river chose to reveal its full fury.

July 19:
Got to Prescott tonight. Camped two miles below town. A policeman came by a while ago, wanted to know what I was doing. Don't think he believed me, but he let me stay. Told me it's all fast water for next forty miles or so! Can hear where it starts from here. Sounds pretty bad. Well, we'll see tomorrow.

It was bad, but there was much worse to come. Three days later he took on the thunderous Long Sault Rapids— nine straight miles of raging malevolence. By any normal standard, Arthur should not have survived the ordeal, but by the same standard he never should have had to subject himself to it in the first place.

It was too far around for any man to portage, and he could not turn back. Once into it, he was committed to continue.

The Long Sault could take a twenty-ton block of jagged limestone, grind and tumble and buffet it, and then, centuries later, spit out a piece of free-form sculpture with curving planes smoother and more perfect than the finest piece of optical glass.

At times, the swirling crests of the current towered over Arthur's head so that he could see only a small part of the sky. Again and again, the canoe seemed to be standing almost straight up on its bow. For seconds at a time, caught up in a whirlpool, it spun around and around like a toy. Often it seemed to be almost totally submerged. There were rocks on every side, above and just below the tumultuous surface . . . all evil, vengeful, carnivorous.

For what seemed an eternity, Arthur had no sense of horizon, of perspective, of time, of space. His entire world was reduced to wild water. There was nothing he could do for the canoe, or it for him. He knew they would just have to hang on together, wait without expectation for it to end.

As many as six, seven, perhaps ten times, the rocks got close enough to wound the frail craft, snapping at her underbelly like a pack of wolves around a beleaguered doe. Arthur felt, though he could not hear, her skin being torn and her bones laid bare.

At the end, the canoe was completely awash, gunwales riding even with the surface, appearing and disappearing as the river decreed. Then, somehow, they were through it, drifting sluggishly in the gentling current.

July 24:
On an island in Lake St. Francis. This will be my second night here. Had to rest. Too tired to write much. Peaceful here. Canoe has some busted ribs. Will have to see about that.

There was a lot more white water to come . . . the Coteau Rapids, Split Rock, The Cascades, The Cedars, where almost three hundred Company of France fur traders had drowned in the fall of 1759.

Somehow Arthur and his damaged red canoe survived them all.

On the fifth day of the new month he paddled past the wide mouth of the Ottawa River.

August 5:

Am in Quebec now, for sure. People in the stores all talk French. A lot of little villages. In the evening all the bells in the church steeples start ringing at the same time. Very nice sound. Picked some blueberries for supper tonight. Caught a fish, too. Pretty good.

From there, it was a fairly straight, comparatively easy run down to Montreal.

CHAPTER TEN

AUGUST 1960 was a scorcher in southern Ontario. Day after day the temperature climbed into the nineties, and twice it reached one hundred degrees. It seemed that the sky had forgotten how to rain; the few times that storm-clouds did threaten, they released only a smattering of sultry drops, then slunk away on the horizon.

In Trentville lawns dried to a crisp and flowers wilted. Offices and factories closed early. People vainly sought a few hours sleep on balconies and park benches. The dew worms no longer came up at night. Storekeepers could sell anything that was cold.

The billboard in the park went unattended; there was nothing new to report, anyway.

During the long Civic Holiday weekend, a young Toronto paddler captured the Around-Doe-Rock championship at the Upper Crooked Lake regatta, but it was a somewhat hollow victory since Leonard Nogawa did not defend his title.

Then, almost imperceptibly, summer began to wane. Partridge chicks took wing for the first time, wobbled uncertainly through the air, tried again, flew. Stag sumach horns turned crimson. Fishermen noted that they had to pull up their anchors and start home earlier as the days shortened. Boys began to toss footballs back and forth, instead of baseballs. The first back-to-school ads appeared in the *Trentville Examiner.*

Frank O'Leary spent the month with his family at their cottage on an island in Jack's Lake, barbecuing steaks, fishing with his teenage son, taking a swim each morning before breakfast, reading Robert Penn Warren's *All the King's Men* and doing a little electioneering when the opportunity presented itself.

Gordon Hastings, a bachelor, attended a conference on urban planning in Brisbane, Australia.

Jim Thorburn locked the door of the agent's residence at Crooked Lake and took Millie and their four small children for a two-week trip through the Maritimes and upper New York State.

Wilbur Pemedash was sentenced to five years in a minimum security prison for having carved up his wife's face. She was still in the hospital.

Leonard finished Dr. Clarkson's boathouse and made a start on the fireplace that George Sedgewick had asked him to build. Sarah and Nona decided that they would gather some wild rice for their own use, even though there was no longer a commercial market for it, now that the buyers had stopped coming to Crooked Lake.

Baz Dinneen turned his attention to such concerns as the need to repave Trentville's main street and wrote only occasionally about Arthur and his people.

"I've said it all, over and over, time and again," he told a friend, "and the plain fact is that nobody really gives a damn."

There was still no official word from Ottawa. No decision. No acknowledgement that a mistake had been made with regard to the Crooked Lake reserve. And no commitment to call Arthur back.

CHAPTER ELEVEN

HE was near Montreal on the evening of August 19, exhausted by his long fight with the river, numbed by the realization that the greatest challenge of all lay immediately ahead. Though formidable, the rapids at the foot of old Mount Royal were not the worst he had encountered. Still, he and the canoe were both battered and bruised and bleeding. Arthur was desperately weary and ached in every sparsely covered muscle and sinew of his body. The boat, its skin torn and the frayed ends of its broken ribs grating together, had been patched as best he could manage with pieces of canvas and glue. But it looked twice as old as he felt. He knew that they had pushed their luck to the limit and might not be able to make it one last time.

August 20:
Decided to stay here for a couple of days. Need a rest. I can see the city a mile or so down the river. Tomorrow I will walk along and find out what is in store for us now.

The next day he pulled the canoe up on shore and made his way on foot beside the river, following it to the docks at the heart of the city. The rapids were terrifying, and he forced from his mind the picture he saw of himself out there in their raging fury.

The bigness of the city was overwhelming to him—so many tall buildings outlined against the sky, the hum of cars and trucks and buses and always the crowds of people swarming everywhere.

49

He saw the freighters and tankers of a dozen different countries tied up along the waterfront, the mountains of cargo stacked on the wharves, the darting harbour craft. He looked up with amazement at a Cunard liner and realized that six canoes would fit inside one of her lifeboats. They knew all about the Atlantic, those big ships.

As he walked past a towering Czechoslovakian freighter, he was hailed by a group of Indians unloading cargo. They were Mohawks and had once made good money riding high steel on New York City building projects. But New York was too much for them, and they had returned to the south shore of the St. Lawrence, where they had been born. They told him their story over sandwiches and beer at noon. They wouldn't let him pay for anything, those fellows.

And best of all, they told him of an old man who had once been known far and wide as a master canoe-maker.

That evening they came with a half-ton truck and took the canoe away.

August 21:
All alone tonight. Seems funny. But if the old man can make the canoe sound again, we might beat this river yet, her and me.

He waited there for two more days, impatient yet glad of the rest. Late the second day they brought back the canoe.

August 23:
She's as good as new. Don't know where that old man found the right kind of wood around here. Maybe had some left over from the old days. Anyway, those new ribs will last longer than me. They patched the paint for me, too. Wouldn't take any money—said I'm paying enough. Well, tomorrow we'll try those rapids.

They made it through somehow, Arthur and the canoe. Plunging, heeling far over, spinning sometimes in the whirlpools, half-submerged, bucking, plummeting. A wild, runaway ride. Coming out of it at last, the canoe drifted like a waterlogged stick of wood past the freighters and the tankers and the Cunard liner. Arthur, his knees sore and weak, pulled her up onto a derelict barge and emptied the water out. And then they went on, under the bridges.

The city editor of the *Montreal Star* killed an eye-witness story of the red canoe passing by, not because he doubted the veracity of his reporter, but because he was convinced that readers would not believe the story.

Below Montreal the river was very quiet. It was like waking from a nightmare and being greeted by a peaceful, sunny morning. If anything, the river was narrower than before, seldom much more than a mile from shore to shore. It was easy paddling, and Arthur sometimes all but forgot the nature of his mission, so peaceful was the gently rolling farm countryside. One evening he heard the bells of three different churches peeling at the same time. One morning the smell of freshly baked bread drifting across to him from a French-Canadian farm kitchen made him very hungry. A few days later he encountered several huge rafts of logs being towed ponderously down-river by churning, but barely moving tugs.

September 8
Got to Trois Rivières this afternoon. Must be million logs piled up and in the river. They use them to make paper in the big mills. The stink is awful— like everybody in the world was cooking cabbage. Makes my eyes sore. Get out of here quick as I can.

He reached Quebec City on September 14, and not

51

many miles after that the river began to change in a number of dramatic ways. Quite suddenly, the banks fell away on either side, so that, in what seemed only a matter of a few hours, he could no longer see across the river.

Along the north shore, which he elected to follow, the farms thinned out, giving way to long, unbroken stretches of spruce, hemlock, jack pine, birch and poplar.

He became aware of the incoming tide for the first time. Its head-on confrontation with the current made paddling an ordeal until the tide won its inevitable victory.

He passed Cap Tormente and looked with awe upon the thousands upon thousands of snow geese congregated there in preparation for their southerly migration. He saw some harp seals around a cluster of wave-lapped rocks and thought they looked, and played, like giant otters.

By then, the colour of the river had turned from blue to green, and the taste of its water from fresh to salty.

A school of porpoises flanked the canoe for twenty minutes one morning, and the evening of that same day he watched a sperm whale blow within a hundred yards of his camp-fire.

September 22:
Still following the north shore. Pretty cold this morning. Felt like it might snow. Snared a rabbit tonight and made a pretty good stew for supper. Am all right. No place to mail letters now.

September gave way to October, a transition Arthur noted only because of the diary. Apart from changes in the weather, there was little to mark one day from another, and few landmarks to punctuate his passage. The last farm was well behind him now, and the rugged shore he clung to fringed almost unbroken forest.

He was becoming accustomed to the undulations of

the tidal waters that were so alien to him at first, and found that he and the canoe could adjust to them. The swells were very long, the crests high, the troughs deep, but you could survive if you learned to read them properly, learned when to sit perfectly still, when to paddle hard. Unless a big blow came, of course. Until a big blow came.

Occasionally, once every two or three days, he passed an isolated fishing village consisting of a jetty, a dozen or two brightly coloured houses and often a cross-peaked church steeple. Sometimes he could hear the sounds of community life—dogs barking, the voices of children at play, someone hammering nails, music on a radio. But, though hungry for the company of other humans by then, he was also frightened by that appetite; like the re-formed drunk, he would want the whole bottle, if he took that first sip. And what he was embarked upon must be done alone.

He did stop off at one such hamlet, a tiny outpost called Ste-Thérèse-du-Nord. There he bought a pair of work gloves against the increasing cold, and a loaf of bread.

The following day the weather turned unseasonably warm. The surface of the Gulf was flat, gentle, resting—almost like the waters of Young's Bay off Crooked Lake. The sun glinted off the cracked varnish of the red canoe's gunwales. The work gloves were left, unneeded that day, in Arthur's napsack.

That evening he set up camp at a point where a substantial, southward-flowing river made its confluence with the great St. Lawrence. From his oil company map, it seemed to Arthur that it might be Rivière Tortue. He made camp early, then paddled up the river for some distance and had a good look around, before the sudden, October twilight closed in.

As he ate his supper, a moth flitted around the glow at the fringes of his camp-fire.

October 6:
Pretty good place. Nobody around for a long piece.
Plenty fish. Lots of martin, beaver, otter, mink.
Saw deer signs—moose, too. Wouldn't mind staying here awhile.

That evening was the closest Arthur came to breaking down, to losing his resolve, to giving up. He knew that his last, desperate gamble had failed; that it was too late for the authorities to reach out and bring him back. He saw clearly that he was committed to the ocean, and to death. And he understood, just as clearly, that nothing would come of it, nothing would be changed by it.

There was, then, the utter pointlessness of what he was doing. And more, there was the draining, awful lone-liness of it, the fact that there was no one to share it. Sarah and Leonard and Nona and John were too far away to be real to him. They didn't know where he was, or if he was still alive.

That evening, well-fed and unexpectedly warm and dry and secure, he thought about Sarah and wondered what she was doing at that moment. Was she having her evening tea or picking over wild apples or haw berries at the kitchen table? What of Leonard and Nona? Was the baby, little John, walking yet?

Oh, how he longed to be there.

There was still time to turn around and go back. In less than two weeks he could walk in the road, turn along the path, open the door to his kitchen, his house. Be home again.

Yet, to do that, to give up, would mean admitting that he had been wrong. If he returned, he would have to acknowledge slavery and accept a slower, but much less dignified and decent death for himself and his people. If only there was someone to talk to. But he was alone.

At last, he turned on his side, pulled his sleeping robes around him and slept, while his fire dwindled and died, on the shore of the Rivière Tortue.

The morning dawned clear but much colder.

He made a fire, drank a cup of tea, then reloaded the canoe. He paddled to the mouth of the river and headed out into the St. Lawrence once more.

By noon, the wind had swung around to the northeast, and there was a renewed threat of snow in the air as the sky clouded over. The swells turned grey, lengthened, grew steadily more sullen. The first white flakes began to fall, soon blanketing out the shoreline.

Arthur rummaged around in his napsack, found the work gloves and pulled them on. Then he eased forward, off the thwart, and sat on the floor-boards for greater stability. There was no telling how many hours, or days, it might take to ride out the bitter storm that was brewing.

CHAPTER TWELVE

SEPTEMBER was a beautiful month in Trentville. Most of the bugs were gone. There was almost no rain. The sun warmed the days, and the advancing season made the nights cool enough for sleeping under a blanket. The big muskies were hitting. Fruit ripened, and vegetables fleshed out.

One branch of a single sugar maple on Upper Crooked Lake turned red—the bellwether of a symphony of autumn colours which would shortly incorporate the chords of ten thousand trees and the notes of ten million individual leaves.

Then it was October. The end of the season was heralded by the crump, crump, crump of shotguns at dawn and dusk as the duck season opened. The early Canadian Thanksgiving. Roast turkey and cranberry sauce and pumpkin pie. The last long weekend of the year meant a last paddle around the bay . . . a last string of fish . . . a last bonfire . . . a last corn roast.

Then, boats were hauled out of the water. Outboard motors drained of their crank-case oil and stored away. Water pumps disconnected. Leaves raked. Deck chairs taken in. Floating docks pulled up on shore. Shutters nailed over windows.

When darkness fell on that holiday Monday, the summer cottage colony at Upper Crooked Lake was as deserted as the government office buildings in Ottawa, a hundred and fifty miles to the east.

At the Crooked Lake reserve, the only exodus was the daily one along the railway tracks to the beer parlours and taverns of Trentville. And there was no giving of thanks. Sarah Nogawa ate some bannock and jam with a cup of tea, conscious, as she was every mealtime, of the empty chair across the oilcloth-covered table. The last letter from Arthur had come almost a month before, and she knew that there would be no more.

As the days dropped away from that month, like the last few leaves falling in the forest, Baz Dinneen's anger and despair led him to make one final, desperate try. Perhaps Arthur had been right; maybe the Queen would do something, even though no one else seemed to care.

So he went to the public library, rummaged through some reference books until he felt that he knew enough about the protocol, and then walked down the main street to the telegraph office. The cable he sent, once the clerk accepted the fact that he was serious, was addressed to Buckingham Palace. Respectfully and carefully worded, it summarized the situation, succinctly but clearly, and concluded with a humble request that Arthur be located and returned with the assurance that he had made his point. As he left the office the editor chided himself for not taking the step earlier. He felt more optimistic than he had for weeks; surely a telegram like that couldn't just go ignored.

It wasn't ignored . . . but neither did it get through to the Queen. Late the following day Baz was called long-distance by an important official in Ottawa, a man frequently described by members of the parliamentary press gallery as "having the ear of the Prime Minister, himself". The caller was polite, very firm and a little condescending. He had been on the phone most of the day with the Canadian Embassy staff in London, who had been contacted by a top diplomat in the British Foreign Office, who, in turn, had had a visit from a senior aide to Her Majesty.

57

"I don't suppose you realize it," the cultivated voice said, "but you've managed to stir up quite a hornet's nest."

"Thank God somebody finally managed to stir up something," Baz said.

"Yes, well, the gist of what I am instructed to tell you is this: the Queen was deeply moved by your cable and joins with you in the devout hope that this . . . this Indian chief . . . will soon be happily restored to his people."

"So far, so good," the editor said.

"However, she feels, and quite correctly, that it would be unthinkable for her to attempt to intrude on the domestic affairs of a sovereign member of the Commonwealth. Of course the Statute of Westminster specifically precludes any such intervention, as I'm sure you are aware."

"She never saw it, did she?" Baz accused.

"The Queen? Well, frankly, probably not. It is, after all, a Canadian matter. But you musn't feel in the least crestfallen, Mr. Dinneen. I can assure you that the appropriate Minister here in Ottawa is fully aware of your concern."

"Oh, God," Baz said, wearily.

"I beg your pardon . . . I didn't seem to catch that last," the cultured voice said.

But Baz had hung up. That evening he drank two-thirds of a bottle of scotch and fell asleep in front of his television set before the start of the third period of the Toronto Maple Leafs-Montreal Canadiens game on "Hockey Night in Canada".

A few days later, October gave way to November. The leaves were all gone. The land, bare and stark and cowering, seemed to be waiting for the snows of winter to come. Beaver ponds were rimmed with ice. Deer hunters saw their breath as they stalked through the grey, silent woods.

At eleven o'clock on the eleventh day of that eleventh month, as they did on Memorial Day every year, veterans of the First and Second World Wars gathered around the cenotaph in Trentville's park to pay tribute to their former comrades who had fallen in battle. It was an overcast and bone-chilling day, lashed by driving, freezing rain. The men stood in their ranks and bowed their heads over the rows of medals pinned to the lapels of their blue serge suits. Around them, the bare flower beds resembled elongated, fresh graves. A bugler stepped forward and tremulously played the lingering notes of "The Last Post".

A hundred feet away, the map on the billboard, its frame slightly twisted by autumn storms, and its faded paint beginning to peel, still showed Arthur's position as somewhere just east of Montreal.

CHAPTER THIRTEEN

HE was, in fact, well out into the Gulf of St. Lawrence by then, beyond Anticosti Island. He had entered a harsh and unforgiving world that no man in a fragile canoe had any right to invade.

The price of intrusion came high, and was mounting with each passing day and hour.

The cold was now his primary enemy. The remorselessly dropping temperature and the bitter wind that knifed across endless miles of bleak and sullen sea held his thin body between its jaws, biting through muscles and tendons and bones, chilling his blood with its icy venom, making a stiff and clumsy travesty of the simplest movement. His fingers, numbed to claws, would not be able to hold on to the paddle much longer.

He had come to accept the snow whitely dusting the crimped folds of the tarpaulin, making miniature drifts against the ribs of the floor. But there was also the sea, its swells ever lengthening and deepening, its salt spray hardening into ice along the gunwales. He knew that it was only a matter of time, and not much of it, before the canoe became so top-heavy that it would simply roll over, or slip beneath the sea of its own weight.

He had not been ashore in several nights, lacking the strength to guide the canoe across the wind and certain that the sea would smash it to pieces against the inhospitable rocks. He dozed frequently, hovering somewhere between sleep and unconsciousness, and in this, as in many other things in that grey wasteland, there was little difference between night and day. When he was hungry enough to make the effort, he chewed a little of the half-frozen pemmican. He had no fresh water, but occasionally scooped up a few handfuls of snow to ease the dryness in his throat.

November 12:
Very cold. Sea high. Taking some water. Can't write more.

Then, miraculously, the wind and the sea granted him one final reprieve. For a few days the sun shone from a clear sky, and there was warmth enough in it to melt the ice and snow and ease the chill in his cramped muscles. The wind, moderated to a westerly breeze, gentled the canoe on towards England. The sea smoothed and flattened.

November 18:
Weather good today. Can use the paddle again when I need it. Feel a lot better. Maybe make it after all! Can't last, though, I guess.

He was right, of course. Thirty-six hours later a blizzard swept in from the north-east. The wind rose steadily to gale force. The thermometer dropped thirty degrees in the space of a few hours. The swells mounted. There was no sun, no horizon, no warmth, no colour—only the swirling snow, the racing, tumbling dark clouds, the stampeding grey seas. It was November on the North Atlantic again.

Sometimes wallowing far down at the bottom of a trough, sometimes riding high, its bow thrust out into space on the crest of a towering wave, the canoe was like a straw trying to run up a swollen creek in April.

Crouched helplessly on the floorboards, Arthur could do nothing to help it. The renewed, and still more terrible cold had taken his body beyond numbness into pain. A couple of inches of water sloshed around his legs and lower body. The spray stung his face, and the ice was building up on the gunwales again.

He and the canoe had completely lost touch with the land, and he knew they would not see it again together.

Thoughts of Sarah and Leonard and Nona and little John ran through his mind, sometimes in dream-like sequences.

In the early afternoon, he took out the diary and laboriously scrawled his final entry.

November 20:
Guess that's all. Went as far as I could.

CHAPTER FOURTEEN

A LATE report of Arthur's position was filed during the freak mid-November mild spell by the captain of an RCAF costal command aircraft. According to the report, read by an openly sceptical debriefing officer in St. John's, the crew had spotted "what appeared to be a canoe" far out in the Gulf of St. Lawrence.

It is well known to members of the armed forces that peace of mind is not insured, nor prospects of promotion enhanced by bringing up troublesome questions for which there are no readily acceptable explanations. Thus, by mutual consent, the matter would have been forgotten, had not one of the crew members told a friend whose family lived in Trentville. The friend, a young radio operator, remembered his mother writing to him about a crazy Indian who thought he could paddle to England. He mentioned the canoe sighting when he phoned home that evening.

By this unlikely series of coincidences, news eventually reached Sarah, Leonard, Nona and the few others who still cared. They heard it with relief but without rejoicing, knowing that any rekindled hope soon must be snuffed out for good.

The news of the canoe gradually filtered out to the rest of the community. Most people had almost forgotten who Arthur Nogawa was. When their memories were jogged, they were incredulous.

"Don't tell me he's still around!"

"Imagine—after all this time!"

When Leonard told Baz Dinneen, the editor immediately grabbed the phone and put a call through to the CP stringer in St. John's. It was just the sort of item CP might pick up, he reasoned: a lone Indian adrift on the Atlantic on a mission to England. But when questioned, the stringer admitted that he had heard nothing.

"What's your interest in it," the voice from Newfoundland wanted to know.

"He was a local guy," Baz told him.

"You're kidding. What the hell was he doing out there in a canoe?"

"If I told you, you wouldn't believe me," Baz said. "Keep me posted if you hear anything."

After he had said his thanks and hung up, the editor sat quietly for a moment, feeling old and very weary and sad. He had to face it; there was no help for Arthur. As he looked up at Leonard, he knew there was no need to speak.

A couple of nights later, the map in the park was twisted from its posts by a driving north-west wind, and the next day two men from the city works department broke it up with axes and threw the pieces in the back of a truck. Baz Dinneen watched them work as he parked his car in front of the *Examiner* offices.

When he got to his desk, he found a phone message saying that the CP man in St. John's had called. He hurriedly dialled the number.

"I don't know if this means anything to you, but there's been a canoe washed up on the Avalon peninsula," the stringer said. "Only reason I called was, well, it looked like it'd been fitted out for a long trip, and I thought. . . ."

"What colour was it," Baz asked quietly.

"Red, they tell me."

"Thanks. Appreciate it."

Baz hung up slowly and put one hand over his eyes.

64

Mixed with his sorrow was a sense of relief, as when a good friend with terminal cancer dies without having suffered too much pain.

After a couple of minutes he left the newspaper office, got into his car and drove through the bare, dead countryside to Crooked Lake. He turned off the highway and took the rutted road to the reserve, stopping for a moment before he had to break the news. There was not much left for him to believe in . . . a good man had died for nothing.

He spoke only with Leonard; it was right that the son should inform his mother and Nona and the others.

Leonard listened to what he had to say, then nodded.

"We thank you for coming," he said.

"I wish it could have been with other news," Baz told him.

Leonard smiled thinly. "What other news? He really died away back last summer—they killed him then."

"Yes," Baz agreed, "in a way they did . . . we did."

"I'd better get on with it," Leonard said.

"I hope they take it all right," Baz said.

"They will," Leonard assured him.

A week later Leonard dropped by the newspaper office to tell the editor that he had decided to bring the canoe, or what was left of it, back home. He couldn't really afford the freight charges, and there was no practical point to it, but he just didn't feel right about leaving it "away down there" to rot, or be chopped up for kindling.

"They say it'll come on the Tuesday morning train next week," Leonard said. "I wanted to ask—would you go there with me?"

Baz understood that he was being asked as a friend.

"Of course," he said. "I'd like to."

When the day came, Baz picked Leonard up around

noon, and they drove in to town together.

"Sarah all right? " Baz asked.

"Yes," Leonard said. "Nona, too."

It was a damp, cheerless day, its gloom unrelieved by any recent fall of clean snow and underscored by the approach of the Yuletide season. Christmas banners sagged disconsolately across Trentville's main street. A Salvation Army band played carols on a downtown corner. A big spruce tree, anchored by guy wires and strung with lights, stood near where Arthur's map had been.

They drove through the shopping district to the CPR station, parked the car and walked along the platform to the ticket office and waiting room. Inside, a steam radiator hissed periodically, and it was very warm. The elderly station agent recognized Leonard.

"Guess you'll be after the canoe," he said. "Not worth bringing back, if you ask me."

"I didn't ask you," Leonard said.

The agent thumbed through some papers until he found the way-bill.

"Just making conversation," he said. "Cost you thirty-eight dollars and fifty cents, says here."

Leonard counted out the money.

"Where is it?" Baz asked the agent.

"Freight shed—right through there."

They opened the door and went into a large, barn-like structure that was chilly and dank after the overheated waiting room. Three bare light bulbs hung from the high ceiling.

The red canoe was in a far corner. They went over and stood looking down at it, silently.

It was a pitiful sight. The whole middle section of one side was missing, and the broken ends of the ribs stuck out unevenly like the skeleton of some prehistoric mammal. The centre thwart hung loose, suspended from the remaining gunwale. The keel was fractured near the bow. The red paint was gouged and scraped in a hundred places. There was nothing inside the crushed hull—no paddles or supplies or the tarpaulin Clarence and Lenora Smoke had fashioned. Everything had gone to the sea. It was terrible to think of a boat coming apart like that around a man, and Baz only hoped that most of the damage had been done later, when she was pounded against the rocks.

There wasn't much to see and less to be said. They were about to leave when Baz remembered something.

"What?" Leonard asked.

"The diary," Baz said.

Leonard shrugged. "Couldn't be still there, do you think?"

"Won't hurt to look," Baz said.

Leonard crouched down by the stern, which miraculously had suffered relatively little damage, and reached in under the small, triangular deck. His fingers found the semi-hidden shelf Dan Jacobs had built and a moment later drew forth a small, flat packet, its deerskin pouch encrusted with salt.

They took the diary out into the waiting room and sat on a bench to read it, while a railroad clock ticked away the minutes and the station agent went about his business, trying to conceal his curiosity.

The diary, an ordinary school scribbler, had suffered considerable abuse from the weather. One of the staples had worked loose, many of the lined pages were stained by rain and spray and some sentences were faded by sun and water and time. But it was all legible, with patience, every last word of it.

Although it covered the best part of five months, it took them less than a half-hour to read it. For Leonard, the experience was somewhat akin to being allowed to study the hospital records of a doomed loved one. For Baz, it had many aspects—not the least of which was a feeling of suspense, of wanting to hurry on from page to page to find out what happened in the end. For both, in their different ways, there was a profound sense of communicating beyond a North Atlantic grave, of sharing death with a close friend.

Neither of them spoke while they were leafing through the pages. When they had finished, Baz spoke almost to himself.

"So . . . there's no mystery," he said quietly.

Leonard sat silently looking at the scribbler in his hands.

"We learn nothing," Baz said.

Leonard put the diary back in its wrapper and held it in his left hand as he went over to the station agent's cubicle.

"I'll send a truck by to pick up the canoe in a day or two," Leonard said through the wicket as they left.

"Oh, sure," the railway man said, "that'll be fine."

Baz and Leonard moved away, towards the door to the platform.

The station agent watched them leave.

"Merry Christmas," he called out, as they reached the door.

Part Two
December 1960

CHAPTER FIFTEEN

THE winter that followed was one of the worst in memory. On Christmas Eve the temperature dropped to twenty-four below zero, and that was only a taste of what was to come. From then on, well into March, there was no real break in the cold, no January or February thaw, no relief. Night after night, thermometers registered lows that were well below normal, reaching a record of minus thirty-six on the last day of January.

It was also a winter of heavy snowfalls and high winds, with blizzard after blizzard sweeping in from the northwest. The deer had a terrible time of it, hundreds dying on their feet, unable to struggle through the deep drifts. Dozens of cottage roofs caved in under the weight. Some small communities were isolated for days at a time. Rural schools were frequently closed. Cars were abandoned in white-outs. Trains ran far behind schedule.

The hardships wrought by the severe weather were compounded by an unusual amount of illness. There was a widespread epidemic of whooping cough early in the winter, and a serious outbreak of influenza began soon after the New Year and lasted well into April. Provincial health authorities also reported a record incidence of both diptheria and scarlet fever. It was a winter of dread across central and southern Ontario.

Nowhere were conditions worse than on the Crooked Lake reserve of the Missisaugas. Their thin-walled shacks, barely adequate under ordinary circumstances, provided pitifully little protection from the Arctic chill of those extraordinary months. Through drunkenness and indolence, some families had not cut and piled even the normal quantity of stove wood, and more than one fire went out, never to be rekindled again.

Sickness, prevalent throughout the whole area, ran rampant among the Indians. Weakened by the intense cold, by alcoholism and by chronic malnutrition, the people of Crooked Lake were woefully susceptible to contagious diseases and tragically vulnerable, once stricken. The overworked doctors and nurses of the public health services rarely visited the reserve, and the Missisaugas knew that they would not be welcomed at the hospitals in the district, even if they had had some way of getting to them.

Sarah Nogawa spent ten days in bed with the 'flu, and Nona just managed to nurse baby John through a siege of coughing that wracked his tiny body, night and day, for a week.

When spring finally came, sixteen members of the Crooked Lake band were no longer there to savour its warming sun. Sixteen out of so few. Old Clarence Smoke, the tarpaulin-maker, was dead. So was Francis Negig, his wife and their two young children. So, too, was Sonny Wobashung.

Leonard was elected as the new chief of the Crooked Lake Missisaugas in February, although word of his appointment did not go beyond the reserve for some time. The post was not a hereditary one, nor did candidates elect to run for office; the band council nominated two or three eligible men, and the adults of the band were invited to come to the now seldom used Community Centre and cast their votes. Despite widespread sickness and the bone-chilling cold, over sixty per cent of the electorate

72

turned out to mark their ballots. Leonard was their over-whelming choice.

Baz Dinneen was one of the first outsiders to hear the news, and he received it with mixed feelings. He had no doubts about Leonard's intelligence, knew that he had the ability to do almost anything well, and Baz was sure that the son would go about his new duties with commit-ment and dedication, as his father had always done. But Leonard would, he felt certain, take a much harder line than his father had done: he would be less patient, less willing to turn the other cheek, less compromising . . . and, especially now, much less forgiving.

Baz admitted to himself that his own approach would have been far to the left of any position Leonard was likely to take; he would have wanted to raise hell, to force a show-down, to have it out, once and for all. And maybe that wouldn't be bad. Maybe it was time for that.

After all, Arthur had tried the other way, tried with all his patience and tolerance and shrewdness, only to wind up drowning somewhere in the icy depths of the North Atlantic. And his death had changed nothing.

Yet Dinneen had to ask himself whether the moderately greater militancy he anticipated in Leonard's leadership would only serve to hasten the end for his people. Baz didn't know; he doubted that anyone could, or ever would know . . . not what was right, but what was best.

Early in April, Leonard called the newspaper office and asked for Baz. Could the editor attend a meeting at the Community Centre on the reserve the following Fri-day afternoon?

"They say I should call it a press conference," Leonard said.

"Well, sure," Baz told him. "Want to tell me what it's about?"

73

"No," Leonard said, "I'd sooner you heard the whole thing with the others."

"Okay," Baz agreed, "I'll be there."

"Thank you," Leonard said, just before hanging up.

CHAPTER SIXTEEN

THE day of the meeting, it was full, warm, wonderful spring. The sun shone brightly from a clear, robin's-egg blue sky. Most of the snow had gone, except for a few patches in the cedar thickets and on the northern slopes of some ridges. There was running water everywhere—tiny rivulets in forest glades, miniature waterfalls cascading down granite faces, swollen creeks, flooding rivers. Crows cawed raucously in the bare trees. The pickerel had begun their spawning run up Eel's Creek. Early wildflowers were nosing up through the dead, brown leaves of the previous autumn. Apart from a few stubborn pockets here and there, the lakes were free of ice, and waves once more lapped gently against island shores.

Present at the meeting in the Community Centre were Leonard Nogawa, Baz Dineen, Dan Jacobs, Jim Many Beavers, who was Sonny Wobashung's replacement on the band council, agent Jim Thorburn, news reporters from the Trentville radio and television stations and the local stringer for Canadian Press.

There was a vase of pussy willows and forsythia on the council room table. Nona, Lenora Smoke and Mary Wobashung served coffee and home-baked cookies. When the cups had been drained and some refilled, Leonard leaned forward with his elbows on the table.

"You know that things have been very bad here," he said quietly. "Not just this winter, but ever since they opened that damn park."

The others, curious as to what was to come, listened attentively.

"My father did everything he could," Leonard went on, "but they won't listen. Nothing is done. So, we must do something."

Baz felt a twinge of apprehension. Was this to be the beginning of the confrontation, possibly the violence, that he both expected and feared?

"We have talked about several ways, these past few weeks," Leonard told them. "We thought we might go on a hunger strike, but we've already had a bellyful of hunger. A protest march to Ottawa? No our people are too weak, and there isn't the spirit here for that."

He paused for a moment, looking from one face to another.

"It is no good to talk anymore, or to go on writing letters," he said. "When we talk, they nod their heads, but they do not hear. They file away our letters and say that these things take time. Die patiently, they tell us."

Another pause.

"But it is better to die doing something, than to sit and wait for death to come. And, so, we have a plan."

Baz thought; here it comes.

"We think that Arthur Nogawa was right," his son went on, "that he showed us the way. We will follow his example."

Baz was dumbfounded. It was the last thing in the world he expected to hear.

The other guests waited for Leonard to resume, but the silence lengthened, and they finally realized that he had said all that he had to say.

"You mean that you're going to try to paddle to England, too?" Jim Thorburn asked eventually, his voice incredulous.

"No," Leonard told him, "not just me."

Puzzled, the agent glanced around the table. "What then . . . are Dan and Jim going with you?"

"You don't understand," Leonard told him. "I'm talking about all of us."

The enormity of what he seemed to be saying went too far beyond ordinary experience to be assimilated right away.

"Let's just be sure I've got this right," the CP stringer said. "Who's 'all of us'?"

"Everybody from Crooked Lake," Leonard said.

"Every last man, woman and child?"

Leonard looked at him steadily. "Yes," he said, "every one."

The enormity was a reality.

"Whew," the TV newsman said, breaking the stunned silence, "that's some announcement."

Baz Dinneen shivered with the chill that had come into the well-heated room.

"Could you tell us a bit more," he heard himself ask, "about how the plan will work?"

"Yes," Leonard said. "We'll start on the first of June. From then on, rain or shine, a canoe will leave every three days, to go down the big river and out into the ocean."

"This couldn't by any chance be just a publicity stunt?" the radio reporter asked.

"No," Leonard told him. "We'd like all the publicity we can get, but it's no stunt."

"And what do you and your people hope to get out of it?"

"One of two things," Leonard said. "Maybe somebody will make it and get to see the Queen."

"But, Leonard, there's no chance," Thorburn said. "Surely, you know that now."

"Maybe the government knows it, too," Leonard told

him. "That's why they may decide to give back what belongs to us."

"And if neither of those things happens?" Baz asked.

Leonard shrugged. "Then we'll all drown," he said.

"My God, like lemmings," the TV man said, half to himself.

"Pardon?" Leonard asked him.

"Nothing . . . never mind."

"It's hard to believe that you can order a whole community to commit suicide, just like that," the CP stringer said.

"Nobody's been ordered to do anything," Leonard told him.

"Then how do you know they'll go along with you?"

Leonard glanced from Dan Jacobs to Jim Many Beavers.

"We think they will," he said. "If it isn't too late."

"Too late?"

"We haven't been a people for a long time," Leonard said, "not since the damn park. Maybe we've forgotten how to act like Indians."

"Well, time will tell."

"Yes," Leonard said, "it will."

The meeting broke up a few minutes later. Baz Dinneen left with the others, not wanting to presume on Leonard's friendship by lingering after what obviously had been intended as a formal occasion.

As he drove back to Trentville, the aging editor felt many emotions. Above all, he felt a great sadness.

CHAPTER SEVENTEEN

T HE story of the Missisaugas'
plan came out over the next couple of days. Locally, it
ran as a two-column feature, above the fold, on the front
page of the *Examiner* and was the subject of a three-
minute mini-documentary on the local eleven o'clock
news.

In the immediate district the announcement caused
quite a stir. People talked about it on street corners, over
back yard fences, during coffee breaks and business
luncheons, on the telephone, at church and service club
meetings.

Of the many individual reactions to it, the most common were excitement, of a kind that might surround either a major sports event or a multi-death highway ac-
cident; disbelief that the Indians would really go through
with it; and confidence that the authorities wouldn't
allow it to happen.

Farther afield, interest was at first restricted to a paragraph or two on the inside pages of city dailies and brief
mentions on radio and television news summaries, where
it was usually presented as a "colour" item.

But the notion quickly caught on with the general
public, not only in Canada, but also in the U.S. and other
parts of the world. As Martin Luther King's civil rights
march on Washington would do a decade later, the
planned exodus of the Missisaugas generated strong emotions.

Letters demanding justice for the band of Indians first
trickled, then flooded in to the editors of such papers as

the *Toronto Star*, the *Winnipeg Free Press*, the *Ottawa Citizen, The Vancouver Sun* and Montreal's *Le Droit*. Many of those editors made it clear that they agreed with their readers. On the news side, the story moved up from obscurity to front or near-front pages.

A national Canadian magazine used it as a cover feature. The Canadian Broadcasting Corporation sent a full crew to Crooked Lake for three days and ran the resulting footage and commentary as the first half of its prestigious "Count Down Canada" public affairs program. Across the country the thousands who watched it were moved by Dan Jacobs' simple explanation. "We are going because we can't stay here any longer," he had said.

Young people, especially, took the Crooked Lake cause to their hearts. Among them were the sensitive and withdrawing who soon would become known as "flower children", the radicals and political activists and the quiet minority who mourned for an elusive quality called "justice". A young rock group in Toronto recorded a number called "The Ballad of Crooked Lake", which was listed, although never near the top, on the popularity charts for five or six weeks.

Astonishingly and belatedly, Arthur became something of a folk hero on campuses as distant and different as those of the University of New Brunswick, U.C.L.A., Brandeis, Simon Fraser, Princeton, Laval and Utah State. None of the students involved had ever heard of Arthur until that spring, any more than he had heard of their schools. But they adopted him nevertheless and made bonfires and attended rallies and listened to speeches on his behalf. The old chief would never have consented to don a martyr's robes, but, of course, he had no say in the matter. And many of the young people really cared that he had died for nothing.

The rising groundswell of popular support greatly encouraged Leonard during the early stages and even gave Baz Dinneen grounds for cautious optimism. For all his natural cynicism, and despite the harsh disillusionment he felt after Arthur's death, the editor did not believe that "the political nabobs and administrative potentates" could afford to ignore such a public outcry.

Baz was right.

Before April ended, while the rivers still ran cold with the spring run-off and patches of snow lingered in the deep woods, both Frank O'Leary and Gordon Hastings, in almost identical language, reaffirmed their "deep concern" and pledged their determination to see that the Crooked Lake situation was resolved "before any more lives are lost".

On the Hill, the matter was brought up in the caucuses of all three major political parties. Press secretaries composed news releases announcing that the Prime Minister, the Leader of the Opposition and the Governor-General were all fully abreast of the situation. In response to persistent probing by the senior critic of the minority New Democratic Party, the Minister of Indian Affairs gave the House of Commons his assurance that "no step will be left untaken, nor effort unmade to ensure that the rights of these Native People are fully protected". The Minister's eloquent reply was endorsed with enthusiastic desk-thumping by government leaders and back-benchers.

Where Arthur's gesture had elicited little more than lip service, it seemed that Leonard's more grandiose plan might well force the powers that be into action.

"Maybe it's like in war," Baz Dinneen reflected to his city editor. "If one poor soldier gets shot through the head, that's just a casualty; but let a whole company be wiped out, and somebody had better have some answers."

81

CHAPTER EIGHTEEN

FOR the rest of his life, Jim Thorburn would always regard what happened at Crooked Lake that spring as "a bloody miracle".

"I didn't think it was possible, never in my wildest dreams," the agent often said later. "And I was right there, living with them."

According to his lights, and within his limitations, Thorburn had done his best for the people under his charge. By inclination, he had a great affinity for orderliness and routine—familiar tasks to be accomplished in familiar surroundings. He even liked, and derived considerable satisfaction from the mounds of paper work that most other agents loathed. For him, the three years he had spent as a shore-based supply officer in the navy during World War II were among the happiest of his life.

Thorburn was well aware that he had been lucky to get his job with the Department. He readily admitted to himself that he had no special skills, no professional qualifications, no technical training and no outstanding intellectual capacity. The posting to Crooked Lake, he knew, meant a better standard of living and more security than he otherwise might have been able to provide for his family.

For these reasons, Jim Thorburn was not a man to go around looking for boats to rock. And yet, although he was careful not to show it, he felt a considerable empathy for the Indians who lived around him. They were, after all, little people like himself, pawns in a game dominated by kings, bishops and knights. It was not their fault that they had been born with little and given less.

In his heart he had no doubt that the decision to make a park out of their land had been not merely unjust, but stupid as well. If the reserve sheltered some malcontents, malingerers and trouble-makers, it was also home for many good people, quite a few of whom he liked to think of as his friends. He missed Arthur Nogawa.

Over the past weeks and months Jim Thorburn had gone much further than was required of him, and disturbingly beyond what was prudent, in pushing the cause of the Crooked Lake people. He had argued too long on the line to Ottawa. He had sent some memos which, afterwards, he wished he had torn up instead. Like Baz Dinneen, he had made a pilgrimage to Ottawa. More than once he had gone over the head of his immediate superior, and that was the kind of foolhardiness that could get a man reassigned to some isolated outpost near the Arctic Circle.

He had not mentioned any of this to Arthur, or later to Leonard, partly to avoid raising false hopes, partly in the belief that a good agent always keeps some distance between himself and his charges.

In any event, it had all been for nothing. Arthur was gone. Leonard seemed determined to carry on with the same crazy business, only this time in spades. And if the Department ever did decide to change its mind about Crooked Lake, it would do so in its own lead-footed way and in its own sweet time.

As far as Jim Thorburn could see, things would just keep on going from bad to worse on the reserve, and there was nothing much he could do about it. More alcoholism. More hunger. More sickness. More deaths. More senseless violence. He could see no end to it, and no solution.

Then, as April gave way to May, he began to notice

signs of change. It was a gradual process, subtle and tentative at first, gaining momentum as the days passed.

Leonard had established what the army might have called a "staging area" behind the Community Centre, a place where the canoes would be prepared for the trip. In the beginning, only Dan Jacobs and Jim Many Beavers showed up regularly to work with him. But before long a fourth man joined them, then a fifth, and soon there were more than twelve scraping, sanding, whittling, boring holes and painting. They usually had three canoes up on saw-horses, with a row of others waiting their turn. The canoes varied widely in age, colour and state of repair.

At mid-morning four or five women, always including Sarah Nogawa, would arrive to make a hot lunch for the workers in the kitchen of the Community Centre. Other Crooked Lake women gathered each day at old Lenora Smoke's house to make pemmican. Nona could usually be found there. They hung the strips out to dry, like the weekly wash, on Lenora's clothesline.

As Jim Thorburn took note of these activities, he also became aware of a number of new sounds around him—sounds of doors opening and closing, of sawing and hammering and chopping, of voices in conversation and banter, of shouts and exclamations and occasional laughter. To his utter amazement, it dawned on him that Crooked Lake was coming alive again, with a renewed sense of community purpose and a rekindled spirit.

The transformation was not accomplished overnight. At first there were some who laughed at Leonard and his scheme, showered him and his plan with drunken obscenities and urinated on the canoes in the early morning hours.

"That's all right," Dan Jacobs said. "We'll see when the time comes."

84

And, as the time edged nearer, the recalcitrants came in, one by one, to join the main camp.

During the third week of April a concerned Trentville hotel operator stopped by to ask Jim Thorburn where the Indians were spending their money.

"We hardly ever see them in the beverage room anymore," he said. "What's happened, Jim?"

Thorburn smiled to himself. For years his visitor had lived high on the hog, building a hundred-thousand-dollar home and spending his winters in Florida, by cashing welfare cheques at a forty per cent discount and hustling beer until the balance was consumed or spilled.

"Gee, Joe," he said, "I guess you'll just have to find a new gold-mine."

The Catawba Trail had dried up; no more drunks, no more deaths along the railway. When the men of Crooked Lake went in to Trentville, it was only to buy groceries and hardware items and other supplies for their trip.

The canoe-restorers toiled under the warming spring sun. The women prepared hot meals and made pemmican. The children shrieked and shouted at their play.

What Jim Thorburn saw around him was a rebirth. The reawakening of a people. A people who were one again. A "bloody miracle".

CHAPTER NINETEEN

Acting with unusual haste, the government announced in mid-April that a parliamentary inquiry would be launched "to look into every aspect of the situation on the Crooked Lake reserve".

The news cheered Leonard and excited Baz Dinneen. At last, there would be some action. At last, the government was acknowledging that there *was* a problem to be investigated.

"Oh, the bastards have stuck their necks out now!" Baz said to Leonard, gleefully. "Good or bad, they'll have to release the findings. If they're good, you can all come home . . . and, if they go against us, the world will know that justice is dead in Canada."

To investigate the Crooked Lake situation, the government had appointed a three-member committee. Baz Dinneen smiled when he read the names on the official press release: Quebec Senator Gerard Fortier, Chief Justice Angus MacTier of the Ontario Supreme Court (retired) and Dr. Kenneth R. Sweetman, Head of the Department of Anthropology at the University of Manitoba.

"Damn good men," he told Leonard, "all three of them. I knew Sweetman when I worked on the *Winnipeg Free Press,* and he'll give you a fair hearing."

Two weeks later, after some preliminary sittings in Ottawa, the three men arrived in Trentville, from whence they were driven out to Crooked Lake each morning of their seven-day stay.

They were an odd trio, at least in terms of appearance: Senator Fortier was in his mid-fifties, short, dark, dapper and impeccably dressed; Chief Justice MacTier was tall, gangling, slightly stooped and, although in his seventy-fifth year, still retained much of the easy grace of the natural athlete he had once been; Ken Sweetman, looking younger than his forty-six years, was stockily built, given to nondescript, casual clothes, and his brown hair was seldom combed.

Yet despite their differences, they seemed to have certain important qualities in common. Like most others with whom they came in contact, Leonard was impressed by their obvious sincerity, their thoroughness, their willingness to put in long hours and their collective determination to leave no stone unturned. All three were unfailingly courteous and polite, never officious, never even slightly condescending. They seemed to be aware that they were aliens treading on foreign soil.

"They're a lot better than I expected," Leonard told Nona at supper one evening. "Don't go around acting like big shots, none of that stuff. Pretty good guys, far as I can see."

"You think they'll do anything?" Nona asked.

Leonard shrugged. "We'll see," he said.

During their visit, the three men dug into everything to do with the reserve. They poured over books and records, talked to individual residents, spent some hours with Jim Thorburn, ate lunches with the men working on the canoes and asked hundreds of questions. What kind of furs had the Indians trapped, and what was the annual volume in dollars before the establishment of the national park ended it all? How many Crooked Lake children attended school? Were there still plenty of deer? What was the procedure for electing the chief and members of the band council? How much did an average family with say, three small children receive in monthly welfare payments?

Senator Fortier was the most persistent of the three questioners, while Ken Sweetman, the anthropologist, probably the most penetrating. Chief Justice MacTier made frequent notes on a foolscap pad and was primarily a patient and careful listener.

They walked all over what was left of the reserve, trying to be unobtusive, but their questions registered their unease at seeing the delapidated houses and shacks, the garbage, the spent woodpiles after the bad winter and the canoes being made ready.

On the second day of their visit, Leonard arranged for them to be shown the way it had been before the government took away most of it. He, Dan Jacobs and Jim Many Beavers took the three men out in three canoes. They pointed out the original boundaries of the reserve, showed them where the trap-lines used to run, indicated the stands of poplar, spruce and balsam that had once provided a cash crop for the pulp mills, and explained how the deer, now over-populating the area because they were no longer hunted, had stripped the lower branches of the cedars in their search for winter browse.

Along the way they stopped long enough at the mouth of Eel's Creek to take four good size pickerel from the fast water below the falls, where the fish were congregated to feed on schools of minnows after their spawning run. At noon Leonard made them a shore dinner on the point of an island at the head of Partridge Lake. It was a soft, benevolent, prematurely warm day for that time of year. The sun glinted from the barely dappled surface of the lake. The trees were lacy with the delicate green of their new growth. A loon called intermittently from beyond the point.

Leonard knew his way around a camp-fire, and he put together a typical guide's meal for them—pickerel fillets sizzled a golden brown in deep fat, fried onion rings, potatoes baked in their skins, bubbling hot cans of pork and beans and thick slices of home-baked bread. Afterwards, there was an apple pie Nona had made and strong tea boiled in a blackened lard pail.

While Leonard was getting it ready, Senator Fortier took a bottle of Scotch and some paper cups from his briefcase and poured drinks all around.

The six so different men were comfortable together on that island, chatting easily, sharing the good food, smoking and relaxing, when their appetites, sharpened by the fresh air, had been satisfied.

"I think it went okay," Leonard told Nona when he got home late that afternoon. "Anyway, they listened to what we had to say, and that's something. I'd say they'll try to do what's right."

Baz Dinneen got a similar impression the following evening, when he talked with Ken Sweetman over martinis in the lounge of Trentville's Empress Hotel. Although far from being close friends, Baz had come to like and respect the anthropologist during his stint at the *Free Press*. Iconoclastic, often abrasive, with little patience for academic pomposity, Sweetman at that time had been the *enfant terrible* of anthropology circles, guilty of the sin of caring at least as much about the welfare of living Indians as for the politics of obtaining grants to dig up and index the artifacts of their ancestors. The intervening years had mellowed the Manitoba maverick somewhat, but without eroding his wry, sardonic sense of humour, and Baz found that he still liked the man very much.

"Tell me," Ken Sweetman asked, stirring the impaled olive around in his cocktail, "what got you involved in all this? The last I heard, you were only interested in three-alarm fires, murder-suicides and scandals that might turf out the government."

Baz shrugged. "I guess it comes with the territory," he said.

"Just doing your job—right?"

"Something like that."

Sweetman shook his head. "Come on . . . you're no editor with a heart of steel. We both know you've done a lot more than that." He leaned forward and said confidentially, "You probably won't believe this, but there are people in Ottawa who think you're a first-class pain in the ass."

Baz roared with laughter. "Thank God for that!"

"Well, tell me how you feel about it," Sweetman said. "I'd like to know. Anyway, they're paying me to ask questions."

Baz drained his cocktail glass and motioned to the waitress for another round.

"It's simple enough, really," he told Sweetman. "There are a lot of good people out on that reserve—real, honest-to-God decent people."

"I've met some of them," Sweetman interjected.

"The way they've pulled themselves together this last little while is incredible," Baz continued. "You could walk the streets of this town for a week now, and you'd never see a drunken Indian."

"So I've been told," Sweetman said.

The waitress brought fresh drinks. Baz ate his olive before going on.

"Then," he said, "there's the fact that we've lied to them, cheated them, stolen from them—sold them down the river."

"Yes," Sweetman agreed, "right down the river—literally, in this case."

"So you agree then?"

"Who could disagree?" Sweetman asked. "But the real question is the long-term one. Personally, what do you see as . . . oh, my God!"

"What?" Baz asked.

"I was actually going to ask, 'what do you see as the *final solution*!'"

Baz smiled slowly, without humour. "That might not be so far from the truth," he said. "Buchenwald, Auschwitz, the Gulf of St. Lawrence—is there really that much difference?"

Sweetman drew back in anger. "Oh, come on," he said. "You're damn right there is, at least by intent."

Baz paused before nodding. "Of course," he said. "That was completely unfair."

"It's an emotional subject," Sweetman acknowledged. "But what will happen to them in the end? They can't live off hunting and fishing forever."

"No," Baz said, "we're all running out of space. Can they be assimilated into our not-so-great modern world? I don't know. Maybe the real question is—would they want to be?"

"Possibly," Sweetman said. "If they could retain some elements of their own culture, the way the Chinese have done, say, or the Ukrainians. I just don't know if there's enough time."

"Ah, there's the rub," Baz said. "We're talking about the long term. For Leonard and his people out there, that means about the middle of August. Is that enough time?"

Sweetman swirled the last of his martini around in his glass for a moment before he answered.

"You know I'm not supposed to talk about any conclusions I might come to," he said, "but, off the record, I'll do the best I can. Okay?"

Baz studied his face, then smiled and nodded.

"Fair enough," he said.

CHAPTER TWENTY

THE first of June came, and it was time for the exodus to begin. The date was not reached with any great anxiety; the Inquiry had gone well, and there seemed every reason for confidence that the early canoes would be called back long before they reached dangerous waters. Baz was sure of it. So was Leonard. They would go ahead with the plan because they had said they would, and because they had to keep pressure on the government.

Still, when the time came for the first canoe to depart, the moment was not without sadness. It was a farewell, after all, if only a temporary and probably short-lived one. And there were dangers enough on massive Lake Ontario, never mind the Atlantic Ocean.

Every resident of the reserve gathered at the lakeshore that sunny first morning of June. The general mood of the occasion was light, marked by friendly banter, some catcalls and sporadic laughter. But there were some who had more serious thoughts.

Baz Dinneen, the only non-Indian present, reread some passages from Arthur's diary in his mind—the mountainous swells, the ice building up along the gunwales, the last sight of land. He smiled bitterly at the absence of reporters and camera crews. The local CP stringer had summed up the media's lack of interest when Baz had tried to cajole him into covering the story. "It's a non-event, Baz. We've worked the story to death."

Leonard Nogawa, too, felt removed from the general mood of his people. He felt the weight of the ordeal to which he had committed them. What if they weren't called back after all? What if they all died? It had been a group commitment, but responsibility for giving the lead was his.

Standing next to him, Nona Nogawa was acutely aware of her husband's soul-searching and reached out silently to assure him of her support. A few feet away, Sarah Nogawa remembered back to the morning eleven months before, when Arthur had paddled away, leaving her to go on living as best she could. There had been many empty hours and lonely nights since then, and there would be more, for her and for the others.

The first canoe to leave was paddled by Dan Jacobs and his young second wife, Josie. Their canoe, strengthened and made ready much as Arthur's had been, was green.

There was nothing particularly significant in their being chosen to lead the way. Leonard had simply accepted Dan's casual offer. Nor had any scheme or system been invoked to determine the order of departure after the Jacobs—no drawing of straws, no calculated priorities. What did it matter? Either those who left first would be called back, or they would all go.

"Well, I guess we might as well get started," Dan said, about eleven o'clock.

There were a couple of final exchanges of repartee, some shouted good-byes, and then Dan pushed the canoe away from the shore with the blade of his paddle. Josie, in the bow, set the stroke, and her husband picked it up. The green canoe angled slowly but steadily away from the shore and out into the lake.

The people gathered on the shore watched for a few minutes, and then in unison, as if in response to some inaudible signal, turned away. Leonard, Nona and Sarah Nogawa were the last to leave.

The Jacobs passed through Trentville in mid-afternoon. As they paddled across Little Lake towards Cemetery Point and the beginning of the river, they, too, thought of Arthur's departure. Now there was no crowd around the government wharf, no parade, no bands, no frying onions or souvenir stands, no Mayor Dennison. Only an elderly man, looking up from the asparagus bed he was weeding beside his lake-front house, and a couple of small boys, fishing for perch with bobbers from a railway bridge, noted the passage of the green canoe.

CHAPTER TWENTY-ONE

IN its June seventh edition, the *Trentville Examiner* ran a front page story under the banner, "CROOKED LAKE INQUIRY LEANING TOWARDS INDIANS".

Picked up by the Ottawa bureau of Canadian Press, the copy stated that it had been learned from the usual "reliable sources" that at least two, and probably all three of the Inquiry members privately felt that the park land should be restored to the Crooked Lake reserve.

The story continued: "An informal survey of MPs indicates that such a finding would encounter little opposition in the House of Commons. Regardless of political affiliation, the Members interviewed all tended to agree with the statement made by one of them that, 'Justice would best be served by giving these people back what belongs to them.'

"Which goes to show," the report concluded, "that, if you can't fight City Hall, you can influence Parliament Hill once in a while, although you may have to be willing to paddle across an ocean to do it."

CHAPTER TWENTY-TWO

BY the first of July, one year after Arthur's departure, there were ten Crooked Lake canoes strung out along the necklace of large and small lakes and rivers that stretches from the centre of the continent to the sea. Depending on the weather they encountered and the luck that rode with them, there were as many as eighty or as few as ten miles between them. Only once did they overlap—when Jim Many Beavers and his wife had to stop for two days on the shore of the Bay of Quinte to nurse their little daughter through a bout of bronchitis.

At the end of the first month the most recent canoe to leave was still in home waters, while the Jacobs were already beyond the great lake and working their way through some of the worst of the long stretches of white water.

By then most of the paddlers had known hours of struggling against hostile headwinds and rain-swept nights of chill discomfort. They had watched brilliant, early summer sunsets and noted strange sights and unfamiliar sounds along the shore. Here and there, hands had been extended to help them—an offer of shelter in a storm, an invitation to share a hot meal, a child's blown-off hat retrieved and returned.

There had been one birth. Naomi Saugeen was delivered of a six-pound daughter on a picnic table in a camp ground near Brockville by a vacationing doctor from Parkersburg, West Virginia. By then, too, there had been one tragedy. Clarina Lavallée had drowned in an awesome stretch of white water known as The Cedars, near a town called Beauharnois on the St. Lawrence. Her two sons had somehow made it to shore when their canoe had overturned, but Clarina, aging and frail, had not had the strength to fight the terrible rapids. The sons buried her in a cemetery overlooking the river, with six men recruited by the local funeral parlour serving as pall-bearers.

Each canoe that left Crooked Lake had its own distinctive personality: Tuesday's, relatively young and strong, with a proud, rising bow, inclined perhaps to the recklessness of youth; Friday's, gruff and tempered in its maturity, bruised, cautious, a little heavy in the water. One would have an annoying tendency to drift excessively in a cross-wind, another, a sled dog's pugnaciousness in taking each wave head-on.

And, as the canoes differed, so, too, did the people who paddled them. Each departure was unique, and each family to leave contributed its own special piece to the background tapestry of the saga. In one canoe an old man and his wife sat stiffly erect as they paddled, lips pressed tightly together against the pain of their arthritis. Three days later a young couple set out with their two young children playing quietly on the floorboards between them. They were followed by Joseph Panache, until recently the reserve's worst drunk, paddling strongly and with a dignity that had seemed forever lost.

The canoes, one or another of them, were seen by hundreds of people along the lakes and rivers that led to the sea. They became part of a collective montage of fleeting impressions: a canoe passing across the glittering path of the sun . . . a canoe gliding beneath a railway bridge at dusk . . . a canoe plunging and rearing through rapids . . . a canoe moving dispiritedly through grey and sullen rain . . . a canoe pulled up on a flat shelf of rock for the night, camp-fire burning nearby.

Interest in the band's exodus mounted, and reports of sightings got back to Trentville. Thus Baz Dinneen learned of such things as the birth of Naomi Saugeen's baby and the death of Clarina Lavallée. From these reports, too, he could judge how far the ribbon of canoes had stretched out from day to day.

There was still plenty of time, he told himself. The three-man Inquiry soon would report its findings. The government would act on its recommendations. The canoes would be headed off and turned back. Surely these things would come to pass. And soon—tomorrow, next week, before the end of the month. Anything else was unthinkable.

And yet as the days slipped away, there came the nagging realization that the first canoe, paddled by Dan and Josie Jacobs, was getting well down the St. Lawrence. It would not be long before it passed beyond the range of regular surveillance. After that, a canoe could be very hard to find in the broadening emptiness of the sea, and the news that the band had won its fight might never reach its occupants. From then on, in the established pulsebeat of the exodus, another canoe would slip out of sight every third day.

CHAPTER TWENTY-THREE

EARLY one still morning in the second week of July, Sarah Nogawa stood behind the screen door of her house and looked down across the reserve to the sun-sparkled surface of the lake. Although not yet eight o'clock, it was already very warm. A blue jay chattered loudly from the jack pine that anchored one end of her clothesline. Behind her, the kettle was beginning to whistle on the wood stove in readiness for her wake-up cup of tea.

The little aches and pains that had come with middle age were familiar to her, and she had learned to accept them, even the morning stiffness in her shoulders. What she had not yet been able to accept was the absence of Arthur. She was aware, better than anyone else could know, that her husband had had his faults and weaknesses; that he could be selfish sometimes, thoughtless sometimes, as frightened as a child sometimes. Too often he had kept things to himself, rather than confiding in her. Occasionally he had taken out his frustrations on her, merely because she was there. But he had been a good man, and she had been married to him for more than thirty years. What she wished for more than anything else in the world that morning was that she could turn back into the kitchen and see him sitting there.

It was a strange and unsettling time for Sarah—and for everyone else at Crooked Lake. There was an abiding sense of no longer belonging there, in the house she had helped to build, on the reserve where she had lived all her life. There was a feeling of being divorced from both past and future, in a state of limbo, with nothing to do but wait. Always before there had been things to be done in each season to prepare for the next. But now? Was there any point in weeding her garden, when she might be hundreds of miles away when the vegetables matured? Would she be there, come fall? Would she be there when winter's harshness swept across the forest?

She looked at the jars of strawberry jam neatly lined up on the kitchen counter. Would they just sit on the shelves, unopened and collecting dust, until the house finally caved in on top of them?

Leonard thought that they would all be back long before the first snow fell, but who really knew about such things? Arthur, too, had believed that they would not let him die.

Sarah glanced out the window above the sink at the houses near her place. So many of them were already abandoned—the Lavallées', the Jacobs', the Saugeens'. So many of her neighbours gone. None of them had tried to take any of their furniture or possessions with them; there wasn't room enough in the canoes. They had just closed their doors and gone. And someday, before so very long, Sarah thought, I'll be closing this door for the last time.

CHAPTER TWENTY-FOUR

O N July 28 a short news item, date-lined Ottawa, appeared in most Canadian newspapers, including the *Trentville Examiner,* saying that the Inquiry into the problems of the Crooked Lake Indian Reserve had concluded its hearings and would proceed to prepare its report and recommendations.

"Because of the obvious urgency of the situation, it is anticipated that the findings will be delivered in record time," the item concluded.

The day before, the last of the July canoes had left. It was paddled by Roy and Stella Kinnikek, their two teenage daughters having left three days earlier. The departures had become part of the day-to-day routine of the reserve, and only Nona and Leonard went down to see the Kinnikeks off.

There were only four families left at Crooked Lake, and their canoes waited for them at one side of the reserve dock.

The agent's house, too, was empty. Deeply disturbed by what was happening around him, and unable to show it either officially or informally, Jim Thorburn had taken his family away on a vacation. He left not knowing whether he would return, or if there would be anything to come back to.

In Trentville, Baz Dinneen's anger grew as his concern deepened. Time, which had once seemed so commodious, was fast running out. The position of Dan and Josie Jacobs' canoe had not been reported for more than a week.

Damn it, he thought, we're going to lose them; they're slipping through our fingers. What the hell were they writing their report on—stone tablets?

CHAPTER TWENTY-FIVE

IT was another ten days before word came out of Ottawa that the findings and recommendations of the Inquiry had been received by the Department of Indian Affairs. The news release pointed out that all three men had sacrificed most of their summer vacations to complete the assignment in the shortest possible time.

Five minutes after he read it, Baz Dinneen was on the phone to Ottawa. Both as a newsman, and through personal involvement, the editor was eager to find out what the report had to say.

A half-hour later he knew one long-distance operator in the capital well. The first dozen calls produced nothing at all. Frank O'Leary had been away from his office for several weeks, and it was not known where he could be reached. The lines to the Department of Indian Affairs were busy. The senior administrator Baz had met the previous summer had retired. Others he tried were away on vacation.

Finally, someone suggested that he try the Queen's Printer. With the help of the operator, he did. A young lady with a bored voice told him that she knew nothing about the report but would check. He hung on. She came back; no, it had not come to them yet.

"When do you think you will get it?" Baz asked.

"Oh, we have no control over that," she told him.

"All right," he said. "Once you do receive it, how long will it take before it's available?"

"That's impossible to say," she said. "Depends on a

lot of things—number of pages, how they want it bound, what priority they give it. Sometimes days, sometimes months."

"You don't happen to know where the report is now?" he asked.

"I wouldn't have any idea."

Baz thanked her—for what he wasn't sure—and hung up.

On their next joint venture, he and the operator found someone willing to answer a phone in the Prime Minister's office. The man who picked it up had an English accent, which Baz thought was acquired rather than inherited. The editor once more explained his mission—to find out, in broad strokes, what was in the report. The English accent was not personally familiar with the situation, but he would see what he could find out and call back. He never did.

Then, after three more unsuccessful tries, Baz finally got through to the Department of Indian Affairs. There, after a roundelay of being switched from one office to another and sometimes back again, he chanced upon someone who had heard of the Crooked Lake Inquiry. This voice was male, cordial and, at least at first, slightly obsequious.

Baz asked him how he could find out what Messrs. Fortier, Sweetman and MacTier had decided.

"Oh, I'm afraid you're a bit premature on that," the man told him. "We haven't even seen it ourselves at this point."

"When *will* you see it?" Baz asked.

"Well, it's not really in my bailiwick, of course," the voice said. "But, as soon as it's printed, I should think."

"Printed? That could take weeks!"

"Oh, no, not always."

Baz wiped the beads of sweat from his forehead with

his handkerchief. "Look," he said, trying to hold down his blood pressure, "surely you people must be as interested in the report as I am. You must want to know what's in it."

"Of course we're interested."

"Then somebody has to read it right away. Why can't you just go and find the thing? Why does it have to be printed before it's released?"

"You don't seem to understand," the man said, beginning to shed his obsequious tone. "We didn't commission the Inquiry—that was the government's idea. It's their report, not ours."

"So?"

"So, it's up to them to decide what to do with it. What would you like me to do—ask the PM to call Parliament back into session?"

My God, Baz thought. "It's *you* who doesn't understand," he said, his voice rising. "Can't you see? Unless something is done about the report, and right now, people are going to start drowning out there. Maybe as soon as tomorrow!"

"Oh, come now," the Department spokesman said scornfully. "That's a bit melodramatic, isn't it?"

"Melodramatic, for Christ sake!" Baz shouted. "They're heading out into the Gulf right now. Have you ever seen a canoe? Have you ever seen the goddamn ocean? What the hell chance do you think they have out there? How the hell long do you think they can survive?"

"I don't have to listen to that kind of language," the voice, now sanctimonious, said.

"Well, then listen to this," Baz yelled as he slammed the receiver into its cradle.

He sat there for some time, drained, shaking, exhausted, defeated.

Good God, he thought, they are going to let it happen.

Then he dialled Ottawa one last time and thanked the operator who had done so much to try to help him. Hers had been the only concerned voice he had heard in the hour and a quarter he'd spent on the phone.

CHAPTER TWENTY-SIX

ON the morning of August 12, in that summer of 1961, Baz Dinneen left Trentville early to drive out to Crooked Lake. The few people he saw along the main street—a tobacconist sweeping the sidewalk in front of his store, a man with a lunch bucket walking to work, a young woman unlocking the door of a lawyer's office—all seemed to move at a leisurely pace, as if hoarding their energy for the heat that would come later in the day.

As he left the town behind and headed out into the country he was conscious of signs on all sides of the passing season. The milk weed pods filling. Birds beginning to flock. The tall corn.

Coming in along the gravel road to the reserve, a trail of dust behind him, he parked near Leonard's and Nona's house and went up the path to the door.

"Come in. Come on in," Leonard called before he had time to knock.

Nona gave him a mug of coffee, and he sat with Leonard at the kitchen table to drink it. Sarah was drying the breakfast dishes and putting them neatly away in the cupboard, and Nona went back to dressing her son. John was crawling by then, no longer confined to the play-pen.

"So, tell me," Baz said, "how do you feel?"

"Sleepy, same as always in the morning." Leonard smiled. "No, you know how it is—kind of glad the waiting's over."

Like soldiers when the shooting finally starts, Baz

thought. "Anyway," he said out loud, "it isn't too late yet."

Leonard sighed. "It is for Dan and Josie," he said. "Some of the others, too, I'd think. Well, what the hell . . . we never expected anything different from them."

"They're bound to find in your favour," Baz told him.

"It's bound to snow next winter, too," Leonard said.

Baz nodded slowly. The two men finished their coffee in silence. The baby laughed as Nona tickled his ribs. Sarah closed the cupboard doors.

Finally Leonard said, "It's about time, I guess. You two ready?"

"When you are," Nona said.

They gathered up a few last-minute belongings. Everything else they needed was already stowed in the canoe. At the door Nona turned back for a final glance around. Sarah had rinsed out the coffee cups and left them, inverted to dry, on the counter by the sink. The morning sun coming in through the windows struck the cups, fixing the scene in Nona's memory.

When they were all outside, Leonard pulled the door shut behind them and locked it. For a moment he seemed uncertain what to do with the key. Then he slipped it into a hip pocket of his pants.

They went down the path to the lake, Sarah holding the child, Nona and Leonard carrying the other things. It was hotter now. A cicada droned monotonously up on a ridge to their right. The path through the sumachs and berry bushes, twisting around rock outcroppings, was well worn, here and there veined with exposed pine roots.

The canoe, freshly painted a bright red as Arthur's had been, was tied up across the end of the dock. Leonard knelt down and put their things into it. Then, still kneeling, he steadied it while his mother got in. She squatted down on the floorboards, her back against the centre thwart. God knows how many hours, how many days, how many weeks she'll have to sit like that, Baz thought.

Nona handed the baby down to Sarah before taking her place in the bow.

Baz and Leonard untied the ropes, and Leonard stepped down into the stern, holding onto the dock while he settled his body into position.

Except for Leonard's hand, the canoe was riding free.

Baz made his aging and overweight body crouch down on its haunches at the edge of the dock.

"We want to thank you," Leonard said, "for everything you've done for us."

"*Tried* to do," the editor said. "I'm sorry it was so little. I still hope it won't be too late."

Leonard picked up his paddle and rested it across the gunwales. "We'll be all right" he said quietly. "It's what we have to do."

"I know," Baz said. It's what we made you do, he thought.

Leonard sat for a moment, as if wondering what more should be said, thinking about the further words he might use. "Sometimes things turn out better than you think," he said.

"I hope so," Baz said. Then he realized that Leonard was trying to comfort him and smiled.

"We might as well go then, I guess," Leonard said.

Nona pushed the bow away from the dock with the blade of her paddle, and Leonard brought it around farther, so that they were headed out into the lake.

Baz straightened up, grimacing at the stiffness in his knees. "Good luck," he called out to them.

"Thank you."

"Good-bye, Sarah."

"Good-bye. Thank you."

"So long, Nona."

"Take care of yourself."

"Good-bye."

Nona and Leonard settled into their stroke, paddling in the steady, economical way they had been taught, and the canoe angled quickly away from the dock.

The lake looked as it might have looked on any other August morning. Two fishermen were casting for muskies off the point of a nearby island, and against the far shore, a white houseboat ploughed its sluggish way downstream.

He stood there for several minutes watching the canoe, then turned away and started back up along the path. It was much hotter now, and the slight climb took it out of him, so that his legs felt weak and his heart was pounding by the time he reached his car.

From where he was parked he could see down through the trees to the lake.

So, it was over.

They were all gone—every toothless old woman, every impatient young man, every dark-eyed child. A whole people.

The few sounds served only to underscore the silence. The cicada, its shrill lament ever rising and falling. A screen door slamming shut in the wind. A rope slapping against the empty flagpole by the agent's house.

As he turned to get into the car, he could see the Community Centre, its tin roof glinting in the sun. An overgrown vegetable garden. A child's swing, hanging crookedly from the branch of a tree. Bare clotheslines.

The pine boughs waved in the wind. An empty cornflakes box danced across an open space. Otherwise, nothing stirred, not even a dog. Then it dawned on him that they must have killed the dogs, each family in turn, when it was time to leave.

As he turned the car around, he looked out across the lake once more. Far up, only a tiny dot now, the last canoe was swinging in towards the narrows.

CHAPTER TWENTY-SEVEN

THE *Report of an Inquiry into the Situation on the Crooked Lake Indian Reserve* came off the presses at the Queen's Printer on September 5.

The following day Baz Dinneen learned that its findings would not be available to the public until Parliament reconvened for the autumn session. His front page editorial in that evening's *Trentville Examiner* touched off a wave of indignation and outrage.

Within five days many newspapers, including the influential Toronto *Globe and Mail, Winnipeg Free Press* and *The Vancouver Sun,* demanded that the recommendations be released immediately, while there was still time to save at least some of the Crooked Lake people. Several urged the immediate recall of Parliament into emergency session.

In Rimouski, Quebec, Senator Gerard Fortier told a reporter from *La Presse* that he couldn't understand why there seemed to be "so little sense of urgency" in Ottawa. More bluntly, Ken Sweetman said that the government should "act now, talk later".

The leaders of the opposition parties made statements condemning the delay, and many other voices joined the protest. Indian organizations, ministers of various denominations and ordinary citizens wrote to newspapers and phoned their MPs. A chapter of the Independent Order of Foresters and Local 134 of the United Auto Workers both issued statements charging the government with callous disregard for human life. And Jim Thorburn resigned from the Department.

Despite the furor, the office of the Prime Minister announced that no statement would be forthcoming until the reopening of Parliament. By then the Nogawas were far down the St. Lawrence.

On September 23, the date originally scheduled, Parliament reconvened. The first two days were taken up with the speech from the throne and other formalities. Opposition members who tried to raise the Crooked Lake question were ruled out of order; the Speaker insisted on following the procedures and traditions of a new session.

On the second day Baz Dinneen collapsed while climbing the stairs to the *Examiner*'s second-floor editorial department. He died of a massive coronary before an ambulance could get him to Trentville Memorial Hospital.

Less than twenty-four hours later the Inquiry report was submitted to the House of Commons. Its principal recommendation was that:

> The area by which the reserve was reduced in the 1954 legislation should be restored to the jurisdiction of the Crooked Lake band council. In our opinion, these lands, and the wildlife contained thereon, are absolutely essential to the continuance of their way of life and, indeed, to their ultimate survival.

It was recommended that the House initiate restitution "with the utmost possible dispatch, and fully restore the lands in question before the onset of winter". The announcement was greeted with enthusiastic desk-pounding by Members of Parliament.

"I am greatly relieved," Frank O'Leary, Member for Trentville-Crooked Lake, told a reporter later in the day, "that justice has not only been done, but will be seen to have been done."

Not all elements in the House were so readily satisfied. The leader of the New Democratic Party, the perennial third party in Canadian politics, flailed at the government for its "unbelievable procrastination and unforgivable lack of conscience" and quoted a *Toronto Telegram* editorial charging that it was "already too late to do anything for the Indians".

The Prime Minister dismissed the *Telegram* editorial as "typically sensationalist", and reaffirmed his determination "to round up the canoes and bring them back".

But the Toronto editorial writer had been right; it was too late.

On the September 28, a sunny, warm, slightly hazy fall day, Baz Dinneen was buried from St. John's Anglican church in Trentville. The service was attended by an overflow crowd of people, representing a cross-section of community life. There alongside Mayor Orville Dennison was the Chinese proprietor of the DeLuxe Café, a softball umpire, the town librarian, the president of the Rotary Club and the janitor at Central Public School.

Interment was in Little Lake Cemetery overlooking the beginning of the river down which Arthur, and more recently all the others, had paddled. The grass was still lush and green around the tombstones, though here and there a maple branch had burst into fiery red, and some of the shimmering poplars were beginning to fade to yellow.

That same afternoon two frigates of the Royal Canadian Navy began a systematic criss-cross search of the upper reaches of the St. Lawrence River and its broadening Gulf. From time to time RCAF search-and-rescue planes swept past overhead, following a precise, thorough grid pattern.

114

But, although the air and naval reconnaissance mission continued for ten days, no trace of any of the Crooked Lake canoes was ever found. "Presumed lost at sea" was the official armed forces disposition of the assignment.

In Ottawa, a pressman at the Queen's Printer saw to the running off and collating of several dozen extra copies of the Inquiry report that would be required by the Dominion Archives and other dust-gathering repositories.

At Crooked Lake, a doe rubbed her head against Sarah Nogawa's clothesline, then ambled down through what had once been Jim Thorburn's vegetable garden to drink at the beach in front of the agent's boarded-up residence.

In the final moments of twilight a small flock of wood ducks flew low, wings whistling, against the thin, orange-streaked sky.

Then the darkness closed in, primordial and all-erasing.

Part Three
June 1978

CHAPTER TWENTY-EIGHT

ON June 6 word reached the media in Montreal of an outbreak of violence on the remote northern shore of the St. Lawrence, where the upper lip of the great river's mouth curls towards Labrador.

Details were few and sketchy. Apparently a skirmish had broken out between some Indians and a detachment of police sent to evict them from land to which they had no legal right. The garbled report indicated that there might have been some bloodshed.

A handful of reporters, in between other, more major stories, were told to find whatever transportation they could to that Godforsaken place and investigate.

Grumbling and disgruntled, they set out, hoping that at least someone had been killed. Or, as one veteran journalist observed optimistically, while uncapping a brown-bagged bottle of rye, "Who knows? Maybe it'll turn out to be another Wounded Knee."

When the reporters arrived in an assortment of chartered bush planes, it did not take them long to decide collectively that the assignment had been something of a wild goose chase. Interviews with the local Department of Indian Affairs agent, an angry police captain and two of the Indians involved in the skirmish were enough to enable reporters to piece together the story.

It seemed that some civil servant in Ottawa had come across a surveyor's report which noted that a small band of Indians was occupying land near the mouth of the Rivière Tortue on the north shore of the St. Lawrence, land to which they held absolutely no title.

There, given any common sense as to priorities, the matter should have ended. Hardly anyone in the various government departments which subsequently became involved had ever heard of the Rivière Tortue, much less knew where to look for it on a map. The location had no basic significance of any kind—economic, historical, social or political.

Yet, once the wheels of the bureaucracy were put into motion to evict the Indians, nothing could stop them.

And so, in September 1978, a government Cessna had landed near the settlement on the Tortue and taxied up to the jetty. Its passenger, a man from the Attorney-General's office, told the Indians, not unkindly, that they would have to move. When the government man had gone, the Indians talked about it, deciding to stay where they were simply because they had nowhere else to go.

The winter passed without incident. Then, in late May, a Canadian Coast Guard cutter nosed in near the mouth of the Rivière Tortue and discharged a small complement of police constables. The policemen, who had little heart for their assignment, moved somewhat sheepishly along a trail paralleling the river until they came within sight of the Indian settlement.

There they were met by a couple of dozen Indians, including a couple of old men and some boys, who were spread out across the path barring their way. Some of the Indians brandished baseball bats and homemade clubs. Three or four held deer rifles and shotguns.

For what seemed a long time, perhaps ninety seconds in reality, the two sides glared at each other across the intervening fifty yards, much like boys in a school yard, coerced by circumstances into a fist fight that neither wants.

Then there was a shout.

An angry reply.

Some jeers.

Some taunts.

Some insults, hurled back and forth.

Oaths.

Challenges.

Ultimatums.

Confrontation.

Then, incredibly, there was a charge. Fists flying, clubs and nightsticks flailing away, the two sides met. Finally, there was a shot . . . a second . . . a third. No one was ever clear as to who did the firing.

It was over in not much more time than it takes to light a coal-oil lamp. There were some bloody noses, some black eyes, some bruises, some scrapes. Two were more seriously, though not critically, wounded: a police constable with some .410 shotgun pellets imbedded in his upper torso, and an Indian youth with a pistol wound in his right shoulder.

With no one dead, nor even gravely wounded, the news reporters realized that their stories would wind up as a couple of paragraphs on page four or a brief, tag-end item on the eleven o'clock news roundup. Within a couple of hours of arriving, they were ready to pack up and head home.

There was, however, one exception among the representatives of the media—a young woman named Sylvia Thornton, who was a junior member of the news staff of a Montreal radio station. Thin, nervous, intense and somewhat humourless, she was looked upon as something of a bore by her colleagues and peers.

As the others made arrangements to get back to Montreal as quickly as possible, she found herself wondering about these Indians. Who were they? How did they come to be here, on the shore of a remote Quebec river, on land to which they had no title?

A few casual questions turned up some interesting answers. The first was that the young Indian who had been shot in the shoulder was named John. He was the grandson of the chief of the Rivière Tortue band. The second thing Sylvia discovered was that the people of the Rivière Tortue were Missisaugas. She remembered just enough from her recent Anthropology courses at McGill to realize that there was something strange about them being so far from their historic Ontario heartland.

Some of the Indian women asked her to supper, and she was grateful for their simple meal of fried fish fillets, dandelion greens, carrots, homemade bread, dried apple pie. They did not talk much.

Afterwards she was taken to the council house, a small, sparsely furnished wooden building facing the water. By then, it was getting dark outside, and she could hear the water lapping against the shore.

Promptly at seven o'clock the door opened and a man came in. He was short and slight of stature, beginning to grow old and stooped slightly with arthritis, but there was still a lightness to his walk.

"Hello," he said, "I'm Arthur Nogawa."

The name meant nothing to the girl.

"Thank you for agreeing to see me," she said. "We might as well get started. I'll just start this going."

She pushed a button on her portable tape-recorder and began the interview.

Interviewer
You're the chief of the people here—have I got that right?

Arthur
Yes, that's right.

122

Interviewer
Why don't you just tell me about it, in your own words?

Arthur
Well, by gee, it's a long story.

Interviewer
I've got plenty of time.

Arthur
All right. I guess it doesn't matter now.

When his canoe had capsized that day in November 1960, Arthur was plucked from the near-freezing water by the crew of a trawler out of tiny Port Chartrain on the Gaspé Peninsula, the protruding lower jaw of the Gulf of St. Lawrence. The *Henri Bouchard* took him, as much dead as alive, to its home port, where the captain's wife fussed and worried over him and gradually nursed him back to health.

When he had regained his strength, he set out for home, getting to Crooked Lake eventually by travelling the back roads, hitch-hiking and occasionally riding in empty freight cars. It was mid-January before he arrived.

Interviewer
You didn't let anyone know you had survived?

Arthur
Only my son.

Interviewer
Why?

He had had plenty of time to think while recovering on the Gaspé, and a new plan took shape in his mind. The government had allowed him to die, or so they thought, but would they let a whole people die? Maybe if they all went next time it would force the authorities into action.

123

If not, he had taken note of this place, on the Rivière Tortue. It was a good place, and he knew that they could all live decently there for a long time.

Arthur
But we had to keep it a secret, you see, or they would have come and kicked us out.

Interviewer
But why? You weren't doing any harm here.

Arthur
We weren't do any harm at Crooked Lake, either.

Sylvia Thornton's mind raced to sort out the story and its implications, wishing desperately that she knew more than just the bare outline of what had happened almost twenty years earlier.

Interviewer
So the canoes didn't go on out to sea, as everyone thought. . . .

Arthur
No, they came in here, one by one, as they came down the river.

Interviewer
Did they all make it safely?

Arthur
Just Clarina Lavallée—she drowned 'way back up the river someplace.

Interviewer
And, all this time, nobody knew?

Arthur
Until now, that's right.

An old woman, wrinkled but still handsome, came into the room and brought a tray with two mugs of tea over to them.

Sylvia Thornton was glad of the break. Without tiring the old man unnecessarily, she wanted to get as much of the story as possible on tape. It seemed to her that she had stumbled onto a kind of a saga, and she had it all to herself.

Sarah Nogawa set the tray down and handed the guest a mug of tea.

"Are you all right?" she asked her husband.

"Yes," Arthur said. "Any word about young John?"

"They say he'll be as good as new in a few days," Sarah told him. "Leonard's staying with him until to-morrow."

Arthur nodded in reply.

Sarah left the room, and Sylvia Thornton turned her tape-recorder on again.

Interviewer
Shall we go on?

Arthur
Sure.

Interviewer
What was it like, the life here?

Arthur
Here? Oh, it's been pretty good—by gee, yes.

It had been, too, he thought to himself. The Tortue was a good place, as he had known it would be. There were plenty of pike in the river and trout in the streams flowing into it. In time, they had also learned how to net the fish from the salt waters of the St. Lawrence. The forest offered an abundance of deer, moose, bear, rabbit and partridge. Cleared and cultivated, the black earth had yielded good crops of corn, potatoes, cabbage, on-ions, squash and carrots. In the long and bitterly cold winters, the women and older children were kept busy

125

stretching the pelts from the trap-lines, run where none had ever been staked out before.

But it had not been easy. Unable to remember much of what the old people had told them, they had had to teach themselves skills that had once been commonplace to their ancestors—how to fashion mocassins from deer skin, how to weave cloth, how to make tallow for candles and extract oil for lamps, how to turn ashes and lye into soap.

There had been bad times. They had known sickness and hardships. There were long nights in the winter when the deep frost cracked in the trees like rifle shots and ate its way in through the thin cabin walls, longer days when children lay dull-eyed in their cots from malnutrition. But they had persevered, endured, prevailed.

There had never been any drinking problem at the Riviere Tortue. Nor any welfare. Nor any passive surrender. In time, it had become a place where a young man could look forward to living, and an old man accept the inevitability of dying, in the manner of his people.

They had been left alone and allowed to spend two decades as Missisaugas, as human beings. And that was no small thing.

Interviewer
Looking back, do you think you did the right thing—the best thing?

Arthur thought about that for a long moment.

Arthur
Well, you see, I think we did the only thing we could . . . the best I knew, anyways.

Interviewer
But now it's over.

Arthur
Yes, by gee, I guess it's over now, all right.

Interviewer
What went wrong?

Arthur paused for a long time before answering.

Arthur
I hoped . . . you see, I thought, if I gave them more time . . . well, maybe we would all learn something.

He took out papers and tobacco and slowly, thoughtfully, rolled a cigarette, lighting it finally at the rim of one of the coal-oil lamps.

Arthur
I thought maybe we could work it out. But, see, almost twenty years have gone by . . . and it's just the same as it always was.

Interviewer
You wanted to avoid violence . . . a confrontation?

The old Indian dragged deeply on the limp, crooked cigarette, the smoke drifting thickly around his lean face.

Arthur
That mostly. Now there's young John . . . the policeman, too. . . .

Quite suddenly, he began to feel weary. From the night sounds outside, he knew that it was time for his bed, time to lay his old bones down.

Interviewer
What happens next—for you and your people?

He found himself thinking of many things, remembering, images tumbling over one another—his father . . . Sarah coming into the kitchen of the Crooked Lake house

with a lard-pail full of freshly picked blueberries . . .
the terrible white water along the great river below Montreal . . . Nona feeding her baby . . . Baz Dinneen, the news-
paperman . . . the big muskies spawning in June. . . .

Arthur
I don't know. I guess we'll just have to go where
they tell us . . . do what they say.

Sylvia Thornton switched off her tape-recorder and
said, "Thank you Mr. Nogawa."

Arthur smiled at her and slowly got to his feet. As he
opened the door of the council house, a sudden stillness
seemed to fill the room. The only sound was the haunting
keening of a loon from somewhere down the river. Arthur
paused for a moment as he heard it, straightened, then
closed the door behind him.